Mist and Mirrors

Mist and Mirrors

John T Stolarczyk

iUniverse LLC
Bloomington

MIST AND MIRRORS

iUniverse books may be ordered through booksellers or by contacting:

iUniverse LLC
1663 Liberty Drive
Bloomington, IN 47403
www.iuniverse.com
1-800-Authors (1-800-288-4677)

ISBN: 978-1-4917-2762-1 (sc)
ISBN: 978-1-4917-2763-8 (e)

Printed in the United States of America.

iUniverse rev. date: 04/07/2014

This is for my parents Jan and Willifrid Stolarczyk, and my friend, colleague and editor John Ezzy.

Mask Of The Kalish

THE STORM BROKE WHILE THEY were still in the open. The old man cared not. While the boy scampered for the protection of the still-distant forest, the old man slowed down and accepted the drenching. The lush green pasture through which he was diligently slogging was not meant for this type of traversing; it was boggy and animal trodden. He had endured worse in the past, much worse. The ache that came from his legs spoke less of age than weariness from such travel.

The storm hit with its full intensity, forcing him to lower his head into the blinding spray, its winds buffeting him like some rickety scarecrow suddenly come to life and stumbling blindly forward. The boy was now merely a smudge against the dark background of the wood. Had he made it to cover? It was hard to tell. The old man muttered to himself in agitation, his lank grey hair sticking to his forehead and dripping water down over his long beaky nose. Oh, how he hated rainy days spent huddling in the sparse cover that the trees provided. Sometimes he and the boy found an abandoned dwelling or a dry warm cave, but this was the exception. The Gods were not often so kind.

He squinted his eyes against the sting of the rain, thinking that at least this time there had been no hail or frogs or small fish. The sky-striker had bombarded him with many such objects over the years. As he neared the edge of the wood he thought he heard a cry, faint but audible. Perhaps it was the boy—but no. He waited quietly at the base of one of the oaks, watching his master's approach. The old man cocked his head and stood still for a moment, letting the rain batter against him. There was silence; he couldn't even hear the sound of his own breathing. Somewhere deep within was the unmistakable inner tone that was the Kalish, otherwise nothing. And then there came a cool lingering haunting melody. He shivered. This was neither Kalish

1

nor Catacomb, but an ancient call. There was a voice, impossibly distant, its words just a rustling of dry leaves.

Spellsingers, he thought, yet he daren't listen any longer for there was a throbbing within, and the Kalish had begun sending again. Ghostly images stalked the tree line: an army marching four abreast with rounded helmets and silver shields, a gaily pennanted tent out of which a heroic figure now strode. For a brief moment its face was superimposed across the sky, growing larger and larger until finally breaking up into wispy orange clouds. The ghost images began to fade, and the drumming of the rain against his skull returned.

* * *

"I saw the ghost again," Parly Yieldshield said. The Deathseer nodded sagely. "I had just reached the edge of the wood," Parly continued, "and turned to see how far behind you were, and there it was, towering above you. It had no face."

The Deathseer patted the shivering youngster on the shoulder. "Get some firewood, Parly. I need to warm these old bones of mine, then perhaps we shall speak more of these things."

The boy clambered to his feet. He was dressed, as was his master, in animal skins upon which nodules of water vapour gleamed like liquid mercury. His hair was long and unkempt, but his eyes were bright and questioning. His skinny, underdeveloped body was wiry and toughened from many months of hard journeying. Now, however, he looked just like he felt, tired and frightened. If the Deathseer shared these feelings, then as usual he showed none of them. Sitting beneath the tree, he took from one of his pouches a variety of animal bones which he placed upon the ground before him—his earth-speakers. Parly watched the Deathseer for a moment as he communed with these spirits, then remembering his task he began his search for the firewood.

In truth he was feeling sorry for himself. The small village where he had originated had presented him to the Deathseer as payment in return for some unspecified favour the old Shaman had performed for them, something about driving out an evil spirit and the reclamation of sterile farmland. When it was made known that the Deathseer wanted an apprentice, one from his village, Parly had been chosen. Being an orphan, he was given to the Shaman by elders pleased to be able to do so without splitting up a family. Almost immediately he had been deprived of his village cloths and forced to wear these smelly, lice-infested animal skins. "They will protect you much better against the elements," the Deathseer had told him, "and you will come to know the magic of the land through closer contact with its animals."

Despite this he had learnt very little of the old man's secrets. If he was to be an apprentice, then eventually he would learn magic, or so he thought, but magic was not something that could be learnt, it seemed. "It's either there or it isn't," the Deathseer had told him. "You do not hunt for magic; if you are the one, then it will find you." And now, indeed, Parly had to admit, magic was beginning to find him, but it was not the pleasurable experience he had imagined—far from it. Beneath the surface, a world of nightmares existed. While the Deathseer seemed to be able to tap into this world without concern for his own safety, Parly had no such confidence. Besides, there were things he could see that even the old Shaman could not. Privately, Parly wondered if the Deathseer really understood the forces that were at work in his magic, and if *he* didn't, then *what* could control them? Whenever these grim thoughts intruded, he consoled himself that the Deathseer was a very old man—how old exactly, he could never be sure, but old enough that any evil power released by his experimenting would have had ample opportunity to show itself before now. Somehow, this time such thoughts were of no comfort to him, no comfort at all.

The Deathseer returned Deer, Bear and Raven to their pouch. Their speaking had been indistinct, and while he hadn't shown it in front of the boy, a feeling of something impending hung over him. He almost felt inclined to close off and search within the Kalish's sendings for the answers. This, he knew, was a fool's option; the crossover dreams were merely reacting to that which called him now. Something new was out there searching, searching like some great eye slowly beginning to focus on him. Within him its whispering voice grew steadily stronger. He could almost make out the beginnings of words now, though they were in a form he had not before encountered. Their effect upon the Kalish, however, was most disturbing; the ghostly visions of the boy were proof enough of this. A premature crossover was apparently in action.

The sendings were scattered, broken as the very place from whence they came. Yet the boy, despite his inexperience, had envisaged such spectres clinging to him like an unhealthy aura. He smiled his gap-toothed grin. They would continue along the path towards whatever awaited them. The voice might be a puzzle, yet he couldn't help but wonder what it made of him.

When facing the unknown a wise man wears his mask.

At that moment Parly returned, his arms full of firewood. "These woods," he muttered, "they have a feel."

"Catacombs," the Deathseer agreed. "This country abounds with them."

"So why is that?" Parly asked placing the wood on the ground and watching as the Deathseer drew two small stones from another pouch and struck them together. Flame was produced. However, the damp tinder took several attempts before it finally began to smoke. The Deathseer blew on it and slowly began to build up the fire. "Perhaps," he began, "because there are so many barrows. These mounds of the old ones contain more than just artefacts and bones. Some used magic in an attempt to gain a kind of life after death."

"They succeeded then?"

"No," the Deathseer's voice was grim, "they are only shells. Well preserved, but merely shells nonetheless. I've told you that magic will find the man. In this case the waiting shells were filled by ancient things, spirits. They can be summoned, but I have never attempted such a thing. Nor will I ever try."

They were both silent for a moment, basking in the warmth of the fire. The rain had long since stopped, and between breaks in the greenery they could see patches of blue appearing. The sun was emerging, drying out their skins.

The Deathseer closed his eyes and let the dappled sunlight play across his unmoving form. Within him a darkness stirred. Parly opened his mouth to scream but no sound emerged. He stared in horror at the dark thing; a moth dragging itself from within its pupa, slowly growing out of the shrivelled figure of the Deathseer. It grew larger and larger, stretching upwards, towering high above him. There was the sound of dry leaves blowing across distant cobbles. Now it began to extend its wings. This time Parly did scream, but the Deathseer's face remained impassive. Parly passed out.

This is Parly Yieldshield's sending . . .

*   *   *

Toll Armon. It is a city of light and gaiety. Toll Armon—its second name is happiness. There are no beggars on its streets, laws strictly prohibit this. Only those newly bereaved may wear black, and silence is frowned upon for any length of time. There must always be musicians, fairs, circuses. Carnival holidays are declared regularly. So it was that the figure in Parly's dream came to Toll Armon with one of the performing troops. *Riddle the Illwisher* was the name by which he was known. He gave them no indication of what would follow. He was as fairly dressed as all his fellows, and with his fate cards and crystal-eye telling he quickly became a favourite. *Illwisher*, they laughed. A more ill-considered name they couldn't imagine. Eventually royalty was drawn to his gaily decorated tent set up within the main square. A great heroic figure was he who ruled Toll Armon, and when he entered the inner sanctum, flinging the flaps aside, the Illwisher was waiting for him. *A small, weedy man of indeterminate age. A strangely fixed smile, as if it were a forced thing*, thought Lord Vorum when he first sat before him. *A man who tries to fit my laws is not yet my brother, not truly of Toll Armon.* Vorum flashed him a *Toll Armon smile*, a truly dazzling thing.

"I have your reading, my Lord," Riddle said, as if speaking something he had repeated over and over again. His eyes were distant.

"Already!" Vorum's voice was a musical laugh. "But I have barely arrived.

"Yet I have your reading, my Lord," he said again.

"Well," Vorum asked, "am I to live a long and fruitful life?"

"No." Riddle's smile had vanished. "You will depart young and reign in absentia."

Vorum's smile never wavered. He laughed. "I understand you, Illwisher, better than you know."

"I curse you," the Illwisher whispered softly, "by the power vested in me."

"Indeed." Vorum nodded. "Now let me tell you your fortune, for I too can see into cloudy futures."

In his sending, Parly writhed in agony. The one called Riddle screamed, and being *in tow* he could feel and endure it all . . . the knife, wielded so expertly by hands he'd thought to know so well. And those colourfully dressed serpents in the audience drinking in his suffering, laughing, calling for more. The slaughterman, the self-mutilator, here removing a finger, then rejoining, miraculously there is not even a scar; Vorum calling for volunteers—there was never any lack of those, to plunge their knives into him, to cut him to the bone.

He was flogged with whips, burnt, then like a snake his skin peeled back to reveal the new layer beneath; to die again and again, always reborn. The cheering filled his head, for the briefest moment blocking out the agony. He gagged on the smell of his own toasted flesh.

At last it ended and he found himself upon the plush rug in his tent, vomiting and reaching out for the crystal eye. It had been knocked from the table by a flailing hand as he had fallen. It lay just out of reach. He crawled towards it like a man caught in amber. Reflected in its curved surface was Lord Vorum's face, hideously distorted but still smiling. He reached out for it.

There was a crunching sound as Vorum's boot came down upon his questing fingers. Somehow, this time the pain seemed more distant, barely a postscript to what had come before. He watched, as if still entranced, as Vorum's boot now came into contact with the delicate crystal globe. He kicked it. As it shattered and exploded into a thousand pieces, Riddle's agony abruptly ceased. An orange rust cloud billowed out from the shattered segments which dissolved as if in acid. For a moment this unchecked expansion continued until it filled the entire tent and had swallowed up Vorum in its enveloping tendrils. Then, as if a film in reverse, it imploded, the crystal segments reforming and jumping back together again.

Riddle lay prostrate upon the floor. There was a faint acrid smell in the air, but of Vorum there was no sign. The crystal globe lay undamaged before him, though now its interior had grown murky as tendrils of orange mist moved within, trying to escape. He smiled for the first time since he had entered Toll Armon, really smiled, and reached out for it . . .

*   *   *

Parly awoke to find himself lying beside a fire. It seemed familiar but the surroundings were not. He was surrounded by old stone walls that were once the inner courtyard of a castle. Of the Deathseer there was no sign. *Where is this place?* he thought to himself. *Perhaps I'm still dreaming.* He closed his eyes tightly for a moment, remembering the woods and the dark shadow towering above the Deathseer. He was frightened at the thought of what might be there when he opened them again, but he needn't have worried. Nothing had changed. At that moment the Deathseer returned through one of the shattered archways, a brace of rabbits slung over his shoulder, his face streaked ritually with their blood.

"I have hunted well," the Deathseer said by way of greeting. "The earth-speakers called them to me, and I broke their necks with my hands."

"What happened?" Parly asked. "How did I get here?"

"You walked," the Deathseer said. "Even those in trance may walk unaided if the spells are applied properly. I have had previous experience with such things." He lowered the rabbits to the ground and began skinning them with his bone knife.

"So *you* filled me with this enchantment." Parly's voice was childish, accusing. The Deathseer only shook his head.

"I followed you at a safe distance," he said. "You walked for a full night and almost half a day without halt. Sometimes you spoke words out loud, spellsinging. Eventually, when you reached this place, an Ancient's fortification, you entered this ruined chamber and collapsed. I thought of your hunger and have catered for it, and mine also."

"So this is not your doing," Parly said unhappily.

"No," the Deathseer assured him, "others than I have summoned you."

"But why is this happening?" Parly asked again.

The old Shaman skewered the rabbits with a stick sharpened at both ends and set them upon a spit above the fire.

"I cannot say," he muttered. "My speakers—Deer, Bear, Raven—are vague. I shall consult them again later."

Parly sighed. He doubted if such earth magic, as the Deathseer referred to it, would be of assistance here. He remembered the darkness that had clung to the old man. "The ghost left you," he said. "It stretched its terrible wings and jumped out into darkness, and then I fell. The dream, I only remember the dream, not walking. I don't remember that at all."

The Deathseer was watching him intently, the blood drying upon his leathery face.

"There were voices," the old man suggested, "the blowing of distant leaves."

"At the beginning," Parly agreed, "when the ghost left you, but later there was the dream."

"Tell me about the dream, Parly. I want to know about it, and why you spell-sung the words."

"The words . . . ?" Parly was still puzzled.

"You spoke them as you walked, though it was not your normal voice."

"What did I say?" Parly asked."

Tell the Kalish man," the Deathseer intoned, "*that the dead will come out of the walls. Tell the Kalish the dead will come out.*"

*   *   *

"We must leave this place as swiftly as possible," the Deathseer said after hearing Parly's dream. "See those towers?" he said, pointing to a line of black spires rising high above one crumbling wall. "Each one has no windows and no door—prison spires. Things are locked within and then bricked up from below. What calls for you emanates from within one of those dark prisons."

"But they're shattered, broken," Parly said.

"Nevertheless, prisons they remain. There are old magics at work here. The stone walls may give way, but there are other walls. Your dream tells us of an Illwisher called Riddle, how he cursed the wizard Vorum by a power vested in him. Perhaps this place was the source of that power and in one of those towers Vorum still resides."

Remembering the torture Vorum was going to unleash upon the Illwisher, Parly shivered at the thought of such an entity locked up and festering upon its own hate. Should it ever break free, the revenge could be terrible indeed.

"I agree," Parly said dispiritedly. "We should try to leave this place. But surely if I should attempt such a thing, the enchantment will merely spirit me back."

"Perhaps," the Deathseer said, "but a man may not walk without legs."

Before Parly could make a horrified protest the Deathseer held up his hands.

"You misunderstand me, boy. At the onset of similar symptoms as accompanied your first sending, I will simply bind your arms and legs tightly together, so that you cannot be recalled."

Parly still seemed unconvinced.

"It is up to you," the Deathseer said finally, taking a rabbit from the spit. "Should you wish to stay here, you may. I could always find another apprentice."

*   *   *

The old Shaman tied the boy's wrists and feet securely. Still in a trance, Parly's limbs continued to move in slight spasms, like a dog in a nightmare chase. In his mind he had already begun the journey back towards the spires. Three hours walking had carried them many miles, but the call of the spires was still strong. The Deathseer removed his earth-speakers from their pouch and placed them next to the boy. Almost immediately his spasms became less violent. The old man smiled to himself. *Guard him well, old friends*, he thought. By the time Parly had worked himself free, the danger would be past. The night was starting to close in, and the Deathseer could feel the Kalish stirring. The spires were awakening that sleeping part of him, and he could no longer resist. He turned on his heel and started in the direction of the call. Beneath a rising silver moon the slight figure of the Deathseer made its way across open field and patchy forest, the ever-changing shadows of the Kalish accompanying him.

He waited there in the darkness and the shadows—the Deathseer waiting for the dead to come out of the walls. He waited—*fox owl squirrel wolf.* He waited—*horse badger stoat eagle.* He waited—*Shaman warrior child.*

The ghosts of Illwisher's past implored him; their voices spoke of the evil contained. As the guardians, they surrounded him and filled the stones—the dead, legions of them, the Illwisher's guild. In the pale light of the moon he began to see their faces upon the great stones. In their voices he heard the passing of the age. With prisons now blown to dust, musty enemies walked free. Had that happened here? Had Vorum and the other wizards once housed within the spires escaped, leaving their guardians themselves imprisoned for eternity?

Ah, but such visions. The Kalish throbbed within, like never before, sending, sending . . . walls crumbling, swirling motes of dust suspended in moonlight, dry leaf litter picked up by the twisting currents. There was the sound of their scratchy passage across ancient cobbles. The wind grew stronger now, a spiralling, whirling dervish of a wind. Above him the spires sang. The Deathseer stepped back, yielding ground to the thing beginning to form within that tunnel of brown and grey. The voices of the dead were a wail—the Illwishers.

The force of the spires began to draw the Kalish from within him, the shadows absorbed one by one—the fox, the horse, the snake, all gone, swept away, torn from within him. He bled, he wept, he screamed. But he did not scream alone, for the dead were being drawn out, plucked, twisted and grotesque, from their resting stones, to be torn asunder and cast within whirling torment. He fell to his knees in agony. The heart of the Kalish felt as if it must burst—badger, stoat, owl all going, dying inside. The whirlpool moved closer now; the spires sucked him dry. He tried to scream again but only blood spurted from his mouth. That too was swirled away, splattered across ancient emptying stone. He tried for the warrior but it was too late, too late for the eagle. His tattered grey hair was being ripped from his scalp. Half blinded by tears of pain and rage, he drew his bone knife free with a bloodied hand. Another screaming guardian joined the orgy of destruction as the very stones themselves began to shake. Calling forth the remaining aspects, the Deathseer gave himself up to it. Like a broken rag doll he was dragged within, his bone knife slashing out as he was lifted upwards and simultaneously sideways. Torn in half, he still managed to aim frantic blows with his knife at the dark figure, forming within and drawing on the shattered pieces of the other things whirling in the maelstrom about it. There were sounds of silken laughter, until at last one of his increasingly feeble blows found its mark. Then suddenly the tempo of the whirlpool slowed. What was left of him was cast out, sprayed across the cobbles with the rest of the remains, broken shadows and body parts side by side.

In darkness the Kalish, wounded, dying perhaps, but not yet dead, called up its final sending. From the shadows a last revenging aspect emerged. In the moonlight the shadow form of a wolf rose unsteadily from the debris, moving slowly at first, then more confidently, towards the dark figure from whose chest a small bone knife protruded. Broken flesh now began to reform itself, flowing together into a final mask. The shadow-wolf waited momentarily for its flesh and bone counterpart. Even as the spire-demon tore the bone knife free of its heart and plunged it into the leaping shape, the wolf continued its attack. The emptied stones rang with one final harrowing scream. Then the spires were suddenly silent, mute witnesses to the flowing of shadow back to receptive stone and the restoration of the guardians.

The Kalish in its final aspect had vanished into the night, but the sendings remained—*a young boy with a bone knife bent over a wolf and skinned the beast as he wept. An older man tended a fire built upon bones, and as the shapes of animals emerged in the smoke, he caught them in a bag fashioned from bearskins.* There were others, many others, but with the coming of the dawn they faded, and not even the whining of the wind through the spires could bid them return.

Voices Of The Dust And Ages

I

As THE NIGHT ENGULFED HIM again, Strieber struggled within his vision. In his bed, surrounded upon all sides by slow burning incense and the Transumi Li, the stone house guardians whose ever watchful presence protected him as he slept, he still couldn't escape it.

A tall well-dressed nobleman was dying in the city. Attacked upon all sides by pitchfork and sharpened shovel, they cut at him, brought him down. His sword was lost to him, clattering upon bloodied cobbles. Now upon all fours, he bellowed as they struck and skewered at him, yet not in pain nor fear, but anger and pride. "To me," he cried out hoarsely. "To me, Rishad. To me." And Rishad has come, to a place of darkness, of cruel laughter where others are mocking this death; yet he knows he must sever the final link. This body is lost. The fine cloths are torn away; rings, gaudy and jewel-encrusted, taken, fingers and all. To die again in Rishad! Strieber tosses in his bed. The stone guardians watch impassively.

There are other guards upon the corner of the street, pike men huddling together in a group of four, their talk a rattling of sabres. This curfew is broken like the others; the city is riddled with such indifference. Doors open silently; eyes are averted.

In the street the fog gathers and rolls, twisting and curling like a nest of grey-white pythons, carried along by the whispering of a thousand unheard voices, a chill wind and damp. Those who have exerted themselves this night draw breath with difficulty, for the fog presses against mouth and nose, unpleasantly clinging like fleshy hands, yet insubstantial, able to be broken apart like spider silk. When they leave the scene, gasping like stranded fish searching for, and finding, occasional pockets of cold bitter air, it is anti-freeze for their pumping hearts.

They pass those who wait upon the corner, who glance only occasionally in the direction of these shabbily dressed artisans, with their arms full of costumery and their bloodied tritons trailing wispy strands of mist like undulating streamers.

When these smoke ghosts have departed, only then do the pike men, in their rusty helmets, enter the cobbled way, one holding a lantern, the others tapping their pikes against the stones before them, like blind men.

The fog appears to be lifting now, spreading upwards and outwards. There is blood on the cobbles, splattered about. There is always blood, but no body. The fog is like a vast grey blanket above them, an upturned river of grey from which something tumbles and comes clattering down upon the street. The pike men approach it warily, uncertain now, the urge to run only countered by the equal and opposite fear of those they must run to—the terrible masters.

The one with the lantern holds it high with an unsteady arm, illuminating the bloodied hilt of a sword; of the blade there is no sign. They look upwards as if searching in the receding fog for an answer, but they are too late, for it has already broken up into cloudlets and drifted away in the night. Anguished stars stare back at them between rows and rows of mansion houses, like so many pairs of eyes.

II

THEY SEND TRUVIN TO ME, *these devils that create this hell,* Veril, the listener, thought to himself bitterly. Truvin, with his handsome face and strangler's hands, his eyes so deeply blue, his hair so characteristically black. In this latest incarnation he comes to me, now in my dreams as well. Am I never to be rid of him?

"Old man," his voice was harsh, used to barking orders, "there has been another, falling out amongst friends." He smiled, almost apologetic at using such a euphemism.

The listener nodded, unsurprised; his visions had told him as much. *The closer I fall to that dark place wherein we all must one day reside*; he thought, *the nearer to the truth I come, death and knowledge.* He laughed hollowly for a moment, before collapsing into a fit of coughing. "See Truvin," he said eventually, holding up his hands for inspection to the younger man, "there is no blood upon my hand, no flecks of lung or stomach lining. I am a bloodless husk, a dried up seed pod. When the wind blows cold and moist from the north, I rattle. See what it is you miss?"

There was no reply from the younger man; his face remained impassive, observing the wizened figure in black robes. *Truvin watches me like a stone lizard,* Veril thought, *that's what I envisage him to be in that other place, a stone lizard, tongue flickering in and out, testing the air, searching for the faintest hint of decay.*

"The body has vanished," Truvin said, at last coming to his point. "The hirelings were unable to secure it."

"Oh dear," Veril almost giggled, "another one. How inconvenient for you."

Truvin continued unfazed. "There have been half a dozen disappearances now, with you the only one with the knowledge, the art."

Veril laughed. "You seek everywhere for your enemies, yet they remain out of sight. I guess I will do for the time being."

"You deny it then," Truvin said.

"That I am your enemy? No, that I do not."

"Then you are a fool, Grimmer."

The listener reacted with unfeigned surprise. Mention of a name he had long thought forgiven, sobered him.

"In a city were bodies are so plentiful," Truvin continued, "to be tied so unnecessarily to such a one." He wrinkled his nose in disgust.

So speaks a stone lizard, the listener thought to himself. *Of that at least I am free.* "I will tell you a story Truvin," he said, "perhaps then you will understand. It is said of the fabled golden warrior Siriad, that while upon the Glory Road, he was attacked by a great bird. So taken by his handsome head was this bird that it tore it from his shoulders and bore it way as a trophy. While he searched for his head, Siriad accepted the gift of a surrogate, but unfortunately this new one did not take; it withered, and upon the body of such a fine one as he, it hung drooping at his chest, bumping against its vibrant host like a rotted gourd. Veril, he came to call this death's head, and it was known to whisper hidden truths to those who had the wit to understand. In time, when he had recovered his true self from the bird's mountain eerie, he kept the death's head, for he found that it gave him wise counsel. So that is why I am now Veril the listener; Grimmer no longer. I have forsaken those paths."

Truvin laughed. "Then you are truly lost old man."

III
_____

HE CONTINUED HIS ROUNDS AS usual. He felt them watching him. They were always watching him, of course, but this time it was different; the intensity of the watching was so much greater, not just the usual hirelings, but many of those he called upon to minister his aid. Even his regular clients seemed jumpy and nervous, worse than usual. A certain amount of paranoia was inevitable, but that was only to be expected. In the circumstances total insanity would not have been a surprise, but they had been bred into a strange proxy acceptance of their situation. After all, the greatest likelihood was that they would go on to live their lives, a full four score and ten, without it happening.

It! The peasants had a special term which they used during their disfiguring ceremonies—the stolen face. Better to live a short, unhappy, illness-blighted life, and in death to ascend into paradise, than accept earthly gifts and then have one's soul trapped forever within the city. And yet it was so easy for some poor mother, upon seeing her newborn, to think that here indeed was an ugly child, and in a moment of hunger or simple greed, carry it to the adoption house in the High City to gain her thirty pieces of silver—a fortune for a peasant. Certainly it was enough, because the adoption house never ran short of children for the great families of the High City. Yet the trade was not entirely one way, for many among the High City willingly descended into the Low and gave themselves to the knife and the hot iron, never to return.

So Veril had his calling; he was a listener, a soother of fears. Truvin and his like found it useful to let him remain in the city reassuring the frightened. So little did they understand!

* * *

Strieber—the last on his list. Mostly they could be put into two categories—new mothers with children and attacks of doubt, or young people, especially handsome ones. It was an old joke that only the very young, the very old or the very ugly smiled in the High City. Strieber outwardly fitted the second category, late twenties, tall, blond and passably handsome in a washed out sort of way. At first he had taken to looking sideways at scissors and knives. But now that had changed, there would be no bloodshed—not for Strieber.

Once within his host's door-trap, he followed a dark wraith-like figure down a corridor of mirrors wherein his reflection was thrown ahead of him, appearing in other mirrors, until eventually deep within the house a gong sounded its warning. The wraith vanished and the pale face of Strieber ushered him within the house proper.

*   *   *

Madness takes many forms, Veril thought to himself, standing in that room once again. A short, withered figure in black, dwarfed by the tall yet somehow stooped figure of his host, he could see in the many coloured splendour of Strieber's garb—a wizard's cloak with sundry attachments—a microcosm of the greater madness that had afflicted his soul. Its source was simple enough to trace. A man of unusual powers could make himself invisible even to the masters. So Strieber thought himself invisible when he wished, to all but the listener, that is.

"We must enter the Spiral before we speak," Strieber cautioned.

The Spiral—Strieber's holy of holies. Once inside he was invulnerable to any form of magical assault. Standing before the entrance he threw his long arms upwards and wide, muttered a few unintelligible incantations, and began a slow somewhat clumsy pirouette, his magical cloak billowing outwards and the small bags of salt, crushed garlic and chives being flung about like demonically possessed coshes. Eventually he completed this bizarre ritual, stumbling slightly as if still somewhat unfocused, and then straightening himself to his not inconsiderable height. He led the listener across the threshold.

Upon entering this folly, Strieber led him along a circular pathway between two stone walls. There were gaps in the outer wall, holes where incense burners gave off a variety of often sweet, but sometimes sickly, odours. The inner stone wall had only one gap and this, at the opposite end to the first entrance, gained them access to the spiral within. While completing this half circumference, Veril noted that the floor of porcelain white tiles was scrawled with indecipherable diagrams and inscriptions, ochre or blood, difficult to tell which. They were much smudged by the passage of Strieber's bare feet. The inner walls of the spiral consisted of a mixture of curtains and tapestries stretched tautly around wooden poles implanted firmly in the floor. They passed through three complete, though steadily shrinking, circumnavigations before coming at last to an opening to the room within.

The final wall, if wall it was, consisted of four giant stone statues crudely realized—Transumi Li—the four faced ones, reminders of an earlier tenant. Within this final invisible boundary, Strieber had restructured his life. There was a bed, a writing desk and a cupboard. The remains of several unfinished meals lay amongst the other debris of his disordered existence. Books of magic lay scattered about his desk. A mortar and pestle, and bottles and jars full of various oddly marked substances, rested upon crowded shelves. Candles and strategically placed lamps lent the whole set up a cosy and conspiratorial air.

"We may speak safely now," Strieber said, arranging himself in a chair and signalling that Veril should do likewise. "Speaking as one man of power to another," Strieber stated flatly, "I feel that things are soon to be brought to a head. Some within the city will suffer, of course, yourself included I dare say."

Veril only smiled. "Why say you that, wizard?" He let no trace of sarcasm enter his voice.

"They . . . the voices . . . you understand?" He stumbled for a moment but Veril nodded encouragement. "They have taken the sixth, last night. I saw it in my dreams." His long arms flapped in agitation. "A sword was broken."

"Another sign," Veril agreed.

"Yes, yes." Strieber leaned forward in excitement; he was visibly shaking. "I tried to raise them again this morning, all the spells as before, but this time I bled myself."

"And were you successful?" Veril asked.

"I . . . I'm not sure," Strieber admitted, "I bled too much. I passed out, I think."

"Oh."

"But there was something, perhaps a daydream, but a spirit came to me, a sad untroublesome spirit. This was formerly the studio of an artist, you know; so he came, merely murmurs at first, then sobs and lastly sad reflections. He painted portraits of the cities finest, yet with each portrait he felt his subject die, as if he had stolen their soul upon his canvas. So afterwards he only painted the essence of it—empty eyes, papier mache masks. He wasn't so popular then. Rishad is full of such unquiet spirits." Sighing he added, "I awoke in a pool of my own blood, a foolish end yet somehow fitting. But I do have this feeling, soon I think—very soon, perhaps tonight."

They were both silent for a moment, alone with interior thoughts. Suddenly Strieber leapt to his feet, all action and intent. "Enough of this, we must prepare for the night." He stalked towards his wardrobe and flung it open, revealing his array of elaborate costumery. "Tonight I will give a gift to the downtrodden and the poor of this city—a party, and by heavens what a party."

"I must go," Veril the listener said, excusing himself. "I have preparations to make myself."

"Of course," the tall would-be wizard agreed. "We must all do our part." He seemed to be talking to somebody else entirely.

As Veril wended his way out of the Spiral, he still heard Strieber's voice from within, but it was lower now, in confidential mode, still talking to a man who might not yet have left, or perhaps to one who had just arrived. As he left via the door-trap he thought he caught a glimpse of something in one of the mirrors. Strieber, his arms outstretched, pirouetting clumsily in his cloak, something that he had found so amusing earlier, oddly enough was less so now.

IV

It was mid-afternoon in Rishad as the listener set about preparing himself. He went to purchase liquor, not from one of the upmarket taverns or wine bars in the High City, but to a decrepit shack in the very heart of the low. Here his proffered silver coin, taken with alacrity by a scar-faced peasant, provided him with six bottles of inky reddish-black liquid which, should he manage to consume it all, would no doubt serve his penitence and allow his spirits release. He smiled grimly at this and began the slow climb physically, if not spiritually, back towards the High City.

Rishad was a city built upon a large hill the crown of which, the High City, had for centuries been the realm of the wealthy and powerful; their great mansion houses crowded together here, grotesque follies with additional towers, spires and turrets. But it was in the door-traps, Veril thought, that one could see the greatest convergence of taste, those sunken passageways where upon either side a visitor might be greeted by grasping stone hands, demonic masks or strangely chiselled statuary, indeed any manner of ornate decoration. Now, however, these were merely signals to a sinister change, as was the poison dart that flies from the open mouth of a winged serpent, or the shaft of metal that impales the shifting eye of a lion, or the pathway that opens up beneath so that a fall into a dark place below will follow. Such were the new ways, for it was but a game to them now. What was death?

The fog followed him home. He noticed patches of it at every turn, loitering like ruffians in back alleys, bunkering down in door-traps. In some areas it was drawn tissue paper thin, the merest hint, something caught forming just out of the corner of the eye, then gone, dissolved like ephemeral smoke. Yet the suggestion remained, born perhaps by imagination overtaxed by a long walk and heavy load, or perhaps by expectation. An arm and then another, the beginnings of a face—the city was full of such unquiet spirits.

By the time he had reached home, which for him was now a single-roomed domelet, set high atop a series of joined town houses that had once served as an observatory or meditation platform, he was tiring badly. The bottles in his arms felt like lead weights, and with the only means of access to his rooftop eerie an ancient, not to say rickety staircase, affixed somewhat precariously to an outer wall, he felt the urge to jettison a good part of his obnoxious brew and carry only what he would need, and that should be little enough.

Steeling himself, he ignored the old body's pains—he wouldn't need it much longer anyway—and began the ascent. The staircase creaked and shuddered with his every step, protesting his presence. Around him a sudden gust of wind whipped up his black robes, swirling them about. A cold wind, it plucked at him like invisible hands, and it brought with it the fog—for a moment surrounding him, a diffuse cloud, obscuring his vision, and then just as swiftly and unnaturally gone. The cold, clear light of late afternoon was returned. He continued his ascent slowly, wearily now, not in the least relieved, bottles clutched tightly to his chest with both arms. With an almost audible popping sound, one of them was plucked, yes plucked; he could swear it had been a hand behind him pulling it down. He turned swiftly, trying to catch a glimpse of this spectoral hand. Arranging the remaining bottles in such a way as to keep four of them cradled tightly, he used the one in his free hand as a possible weapon. But he saw nothing. It was then that the second bottle was snatched; this time the tug was so strong that it almost made him topple over, and it did make him release his free hand and grasp at the railing for support. The whole structure shifted disconcertingly while Veril's eyes stayed upon the bottle he had just released as it spiralled downwards, seemingly in slow motion, to shatter at last upon the cobbles below, spraying glass and bloody liquid out across the street. *It could have been me,* he thought, *and it still might be,* he added to himself as a reminder.

From somewhere there came a sound not unlike the buzzing of a swarm of bees, soft at first and then louder, then soft again. Veril continued climbing, certain only that he must get to the top as swiftly as possible. Attacked by sudden silence, he ducked his head in premonition. A bottle smashed itself against the side of the wall and splattered him with glass; its contents flowed upon the scum-encrusted stone, sizzling evilly. *Missed me,* he thought, *you've got just one more chance.* Within moments he had reached the top of the roof, and was contemplating a final dash, if his old legs could take it, to the safety of his dome. What he saw upon arrival, if not exactly a relief, at least made haste less necessary. The other bottle had been cracked open upon the roof, as if in some bizarre naming ceremony, or as a signal of things yet to come. Should he have needed any confirmation, he remained amongst the unforgiven.

V

"BENEATH THIS CITY OF MAN there is another, a perfect place, a place such as the ancients knew."

The voice was wise, assured. Memories he thought long-erased, now returned. The fire in his throat had cooled somewhat, but the headache remained. The room shifted eerily; he found it hard to focus. The voice continued unabated. He tried to block it out by taking another swig.

"Ley lines, where the fixing of place first began, the source of our magic."

The source! Veril laughed to himself hollowly; the bitter taste lingered.

Sitting propped upon his old bed in the spartanly furnished dome, he looked and felt like an aging wino. The window slots were boarded up and the door crack stuffed with cloth. Despite this, wisps of fog continued to seep within, gathering in the shadows cast from his single candle. He lifted one withered hand and looked between its spread fingers at the interesting shapes developing. He laughed again and took another shot. Somewhere other voices were calling, a buzzing noise like a swarm of bees or wasps. He couldn't escape it this time; his head was the dome and these insects were battering from within. It would have been easy, he thought, so easy to recant and rejoin the others, yet images of stone lizards remained, as an echo. They were all echoes really, remnants of a past that refused to die. Some had been his friends once, but not Truvin, he decided, never he.

Another swig.

The amount of fog within the dome had increased again. Part of the cloth he had used to plug the crack beneath the door was gone, apparently pulled beneath and out by invisible hands. The fog was pouring in through this gap now. He thought briefly about getting up and trying to plug this hole in the dike, but decided against it. The fog had begun to curl itself into primitive approximations of limbs, which periodically broke up and restructured in a continuing pattern. He watched passively, aware somehow that this was merely a prelude, an entrée. There was no fear, only resignation, and perhaps a touch of drink-induced euphoria.

Suddenly it began in earnest. The diffuse cloud of fog collapsed in upon itself, leaving him momentarily disoriented. Blinking his eyes firmly, he saw at last what it was that hung in the centre of his room—the sword of Damocles—without its hilt, a blood encrusted blade; it glinted in the candlelight, yet it moved neither towards him nor away.

The fog rushed through the crack now, as if drawn by suction to the space around the blade, forming, by fingers first, a pair of gripping hands. No mere approximations these, they were real. He saw the dirt beneath the fingernails and the veins standing out upon their wrists; blood dripped from where they gripped the sharp blade. He remembered those bodies which had vanished, and now understood why Truvin hadn't been able to locate them. Ever longer the wrists grew, now into brawny forearms, and still the fog was syphoning through the crack, drawn into thin threads and twisting like cotton into a weaving machine. Veril was half expecting the entire body to form before the attack came, so he was somewhat surprised when the disembodied forearms, with their crazily twisting ribbons of grey, began to move purposely towards him, the sacrificial blade being lifted high. Even in his inebriated state he was able to scramble to the far side of his bed, bottle still clutched in one hand as the blade descended, just missing him and embedding itself in his mattress. He was backed up against the wall now, in a small space between his bed and bedside table which still held the candle and two other bottles, one empty, the other as yet unopened. The blade was plucked free of the mattress by the spectre which now, broad shouldered though still headless, reminded him curiously of the tale of Siriad.

As Veril watched, the twin ribbons joined as one, and, as if in a sense of moment, the spectre halted to allow the unforgiven one a glimpse of the face of his executioner. He caught sight of the madly staring eyes as for the first time a genuine fear gripped him, a fear for his moral soul. The blade darted at his chest in triumph. He cringed downward, throwing up his hands and the bottle in one, as a last form of protection. The sudden jerk sent out a jet of red-black liquid to intersect with the spectre mid-lunge—a lazy red stripe from wrists to left shoulder. It came apart like fairy floss, sizzling and dissolving into a greenish puke that scattered out across his bedclothes and the wall.

Veril looked up in surprise, wondering at the source of his salvation. The truth not having yet dawned; he watched as the shattered remains of the spectre, now having retreated to the middle of the room, attempted to repair itself. The fog ribbons had divided into a dozen smaller versions, like frantic spiders trying to reweave a broken web.

Veril clambered to his feet, noticing that he still held his wine bottle—a bitter brew. With a sudden smile of realization, he placed his thumb over the opening and began a violent shaking. He felt the anger within the bottle. The pressure against his thumb increased mightily; still he continued shaking, watching the spectre all the while as it again neared something like completion. At that moment Veril, placing one foot up upon the bed and aiming carefully, extinguished that particular fire once and for all. Fog ribbons retreated in agonised writhing, like snakes with their heads removed. With the bottle still held in his hands, like the weapon it now was, he flung open the door and confronted the night beyond.

Nothing . . . The remains of passing fog banks drifted aimlessly in small patches, while in the distance, in the direction of the High City, a great cloud was gathering.

VI

THE COOL, CRISP NIGHT AIR revived him somewhat, and it was that, as much as an understandable reluctance to return to where the remains of the fog spectre lay splattered across his room, that brought Veril down to the street level. Grabbing the last unopened bottle as insurance, he had decided to make for the Low City and wait for the morning and any degree of safety that it might bring. The further away from the High City and its problems this night, the better, Veril thought. He had barely taken a few steps in this direction, however, before he encountered Strieber at the head of a large band of people, both peasant and noble, heading in the opposite direction. The tall would-be wizard was dressed in dark purple robes with silver pentagrams and a fringe of golden corn cobs. His bare feet were bloodied red in the glow of the torches held by his acolytes, while behind them in seemingly endless ragged lines, the people followed. Others were joining them even as he watched, leaving their door-traps and following the bizarre procession as it wended its way towards the High City, still locked, as it was, in its pall of grey. What strange compulsion drove them, Veril wondered, what fey dreams.

Strieber's eyes were locked as he kicked his heels and twisted in dainty pirouettes, fluid and smooth like a dancer. The corn cobs spun with him, a rainbow of gold.

"To me," he cried. "Rishad, to me—to me." And Rishad came.

Veril found himself pressed up against stone at their passing, and when at last they were gone, all except those stragglers, the aged and infirm, he opened up his last bottle, took a stiffening swig, and followed them.

The fog began to lift as they drew nearer the heart of the High City, the domain of the masters. It lifted from their towers and their spires and their domes; it left via door-trap, window and skylight, until only their ruins remained—broken towers, cracked domes, shattered windows. Reflected in the newly born starlight was a ghost city. It was as if two hundred years of time had passed in just one moment. Veril saw, but didn't see. About him, cheering had started.

Strieber began a spin quicker and tighter than before; like a top his outline was blurring and shifting. Flames from the surrounding torches were absorbed into this spiral, but still it continued.

* * *

The fog rolled in above them, as a blanket of grey. So swiftly it moved, yet it dropped many things as it passed—gold coins, jewellery, clothing, small things. Yet larger items fell as well. Lavish furnishings crashed down amongst the revellers who dashed about wildly, scavenging as much as they could while trying not to be struck by falling four-posters or heavy statuary.

Through all this surrounding chaos Veril stood quietly, aware of other places, other times. From that dark place they called to him for his help, his brothers and sisters, even Truvin. *Too late,* he thought sadly. *Far too late.*

Out upon the streets, people still picking through the wreckage looked to the skies for further gifts, as one by one they felt something like rain strike their faces. Then a woman wiped it clear with her hand and screamed. This scream was soon taken up. Other things were falling out of the night now, bouncing off shattered furniture and crashing against blood spattered cobbles. Upon the street and all about him the screaming continued, but for Veril there were only the echoes.

And Some Travellers Return

(THE DEAD)

I

TREVIS

THE OLD SOLDIER STOOD AT the window and peered out into the evening shadows. He motioned to me with one withered hand.

"Look," he said, "they are here now."

As I approached the window he grasped my shoulder, propelling me towards the glass.

"All the merchants of Tire, the fat and the thin, the eyeless and the disembowelled, see, see . . ."

His hand upon my shoulder clasped ever firmer, digging into my skin. Still I said nothing, watching the shadows.

"They follow me all the while. They track my steps." His voice was breaking now. "Always more. Legions of the dead; women, children. See how they summon me."

"For all your sins," I said softly.

"No." His voice was bitter. "I did kill, yes I did, but not this . . ."

"The sins of the many vested upon the few." This was not my voice nor his, yet I didn't have to turn to see who had joined us; Keldon's reflection in the ancient glass was distorted, yet unmistakable. The old soldier hadn't noticed his arrival and rambled on as old soldiers are wont.

I held myself upright and continued to look outwards into a darkening street. The shadows were lengthening and swallowing up the light. There was nothing else there; when I turned I wanted to be certain in myself that this was the case. I squinted and tried to balance out the effects of the glass; momentarily, the street seemed to leap up at me, the shadows rolled away. I could see the very cracks in the cobbles, wheel ruts, scuffing from the passage of feet, nothing else. Dust motes danced in a beam of late afternoon sunshine; they formed no discernible pattern. I closed my eyes. The old soldier too had fallen silent, lost within his memories or his nightmares. I sighed and turned to face Keldon. "There is nothing here for me," I said with finality, the verbal equivalent of the executioner's axe. Yet the corpse refused to lie still.

"You are mistaken," Keldon spluttered. "If you would look again you'd see what I . . ."

"No!" I drove this dagger into his heart. "Understand me, Keldon; all I have seen here is an empty courtyard and silent rooms. You have shown me all that I need see, now, or ever."

"There is still coin to be made from murder in Verinkad, if what one hears is correct." The old soldier was standing behind me. Neither myself nor Keldon had noticed his leaving the window, but a cold chill preceded him.

"Feel it, did you?"

"What?"

"Their hands. They reached out and touched you."

He suddenly didn't seem so old and harmless. I remembered the surprising power of his fingers. His face was sharp and hard—madness glittered in his eyes.

Keldon meanwhile had backed off, but his vast bulk now blocked the corridor, a fat man in the eye of a needle. I remembered however that he too had killed, though mostly by proxy—his hand had gifted the gold or mixed the poison.

"This place is clean. If there be demons here, they be the fruits of your own mind's eye. You must look to yourselves; the answer lies within, not with the likes of me."

I walked away now, leaving the old soldier at his doorway; his eyes burnt into my back. Keldon the fat pressed himself against the wall as I passed—a great cancerous bulk.

"You did not answer my charge, bonegrinder." The soldier's voice hung in the air, like an unexplained roll of thunder on a clear summer day.

As I retraced my steps down a staircase and onto the ground level, another of them was waiting for me at the base, in their red robes; his frightened eyes watched me as I pushed past. I gave him barely a glance, as I made for the safety of the street, those words still reverberating—*there is still coin to be made from murder in Verinkad.*

As I passed beneath the old soldier's window I glanced up to see if he still watched me, but there were only formless shadows—darkness upon darkness. I walked on. Soon it would be night.

*   *   *

"Vertellen's followers fill the city, "Lanting said with distaste. "Worshipers of the hard road may they be, but there are as many in the taverns and brothels as the waiting houses; perhaps it is this that has disturbed the old gods."

He was hoping that I would confirm this phenomenon. "The old gods, as you term them, are no more than broken stones; at least Vertellen's followers worship a living, breathing man, though he is, of course, a charlatan."

Lanting looked at me as if I had gone mad; he was about to splutter some inane defence of his gods or even more wearisome condemnation of me, when I raised a hand. "Hear me out, Brother Lanting," I said, "for I bring news of the dead risen up, of evil men gathered together beneath a sign of the true guild."

"How can this be? "He was incredulous.

"Keldon the fat, Hettelshrick of the Assassin's Guild and many others of the like have occupied buildings within the Sortileger's Way, and decreed them waiting houses."

"What!" Brother Lanting had turned white with rage and his hands were shaking.

"They claim the sacrament of the Brotherhood. They offer themselves before the gods, in the hope that their ghost burdens will be absolved, their tears of repentance shall wash clear the mists of indifference from the eye . . ."

"Enough!" Lanting's face had hardened into a fair representation of one of his stony masters. "What have you to do with this abomination, bonegrinder? You speak as if their mouthpiece."

"I speak only as a friend of the Brotherhood." I managed to hold a straight face as I said this, but Lanting would have none of it.

"You are a troublemaker, Trevis. If it should prove that you are behind this latest insult to the guild . . ."

"Yes?" I provoked him. "And what then will you do? Place upon me a curse? Bring me out in boils, or afflict me with ravens? Rain me with stones?"

"The gods will not be mocked," he warned. "I have said this before . . ."

"And no doubt you will say it again, but you lose sight of the present to blunder foolishly about in the past. While you threaten me hollowly, there are others who stink with the foul odour of corruption, who now fawn before the feet of your gods. They are not my journeymen, Lanting. Perchance they be yours?"

"No, never," he replied.

"Then in this at least we are agreed; in this we are brothers."

He rose now from his simple pinewood desk and stood with his back to me—a large man, hewn from some great stone. Picture him holding an axe, the executioner if you will, now holding ancient parchment, turning it lovingly, gently, within his great hands—more difficult, to be sure, but closer.

He had come to whatever decision he needed to make, and turned back to face me. He didn't try to hide his dislike, with the carefully neutral face that was his usual guise.

"What is your interest in this matter, Trevis? You are not my brother and never will be. We both know that."

I nodded courteously, deciding not to provoke him further. There was something in his manner that spoke of older things, of kinships beyond those of guild and blood.

"There is evil here," I said quietly. "These men, I am troubled by their hauntings."

"Why? Were you threatened in some way?"

I admired his prescience and nodded. "Absurd to be sure, yet there was this old butcher, a veteran of many a murderous campaign. Perchance you've heard of the siege of Tire?"

Lanting nodded. "A particularly nasty affair, merchants and nobles cut open by soldiers in the search for swallowed valuables; a low point in the histories of the lands, but alas not an isolated case."

"Perhaps not, but it seems his sins have come back to haunt him. Or at least he thinks they have. Yet I found nothing."

Lanting shook his head. "I don't understand; usually you are scornful of such things."

"You are right, of course; normally I would have brushed it aside, and so I did, to begin with, but there have been strange happenings since."

"Street deaths," Lanting said and nodded his understanding. "Yes, we suspect Vertellen's drunken followers."

"I have been called upon on four different occasions," I told him. "Each time I had to prepare the bodies, as street law decrees."

Lanting, despite himself, grimaced. "You must do as you see fit, I suppose." He was noticeably uncomfortable.

"You understand the processes involved?"

"I have an inkling," he admitted.

"It isn't pretty," I agreed, "but when a body is found between the hours of midnight and six, I must be called in."

"Tradition . . ." Lanting began.

But I interrupted him vigorously. "Yes, tradition, folklore, superstition, call it what you will, but there is more to it than just that. Fear, Brother Lanting, fear of the dead hand reaching out with clawed fingers, to tear at the throat and heart. On the streets,

Brother Lanting, when the fog rolls in and the curfew bell tolls for the final time, then you understand my Verinkad, Brother Lanting. In the hours between twelve and six, I am all there is."

"Yet for all this you claim to be afraid of the threats of a bluff brigand." Lanting seemed unconvinced.

"Not for myself. It was the city he was referring to, not so much a threat really as just a statement of fact—murder in Verinkad. His eyes, Lanting, the abyss be my witness, to have seen his eyes." I fell silent.

Lanting stood for a moment. "They have taken upon themselves the status of a waiting house, and of this you are sure?"

I nodded. "They reach out for your broken stones, Brother Lanting, and I fear they murder in misguided sacrifice."

"I am left with little choice," Lanting intoned solemnly.

"The sword . . . ?" I asked.

"Unsheathe it and return here at midnight; the guild shall provide two dozen Brothers. We shall cleanse this stain from our midst."

"I shall bring the salt and ashes," I said, still half expecting him to refuse, or at least put up an objection.

"Quite so," said Brother Lanting.

(BROKEN STONES)

II

LANTING

HAVING SENT WORD TO THAT trick master Vertellen that I wished to see him, I received word late in the afternoon—I had been granted an audience, an audience! The man's effrontery knows no bounds.

I proceeded forthwith to the slightly down at heel boarding house he had taken as his seat of occupation within Verinkad.

I was shown into a small, unadorned room by one of his lackeys, where I would have to wait for His Servitude as they called him. Several cushions were placed atop a rug depicting the march of the guildsmen upon the Mad Crusade. The rug was an especially fine specimen, though, as with most things to do with Vertellen, it was most certainly a fake. The faces of the guildsmen were filled not with pain, weariness and fear, but a certain holy rapture, or perhaps they were simply drunk. If this was so, then it was indeed a true representation of the second Crusade, if not the first.

"Brother Lanting, what a fine thing it is that I may greet a fellow traveller upon this, our great journey." Vertellen was a small thin man with dark wavy hair, and the mischievous smile of a man who knows he is pulling off a great dupe, but that nobody can touch him—his green eyes sparkled.

By god, does he really expect me to kneel and kiss his hand? I thought, half in wonder at his sheer cheek, and half in irritation at the calculated insult? I felt I had been annoyed enough for one day (by that bonegrinder Trevis) and so stood to my full, not inconsiderable height, and favoured him with a withering stare.

He smiled with an unrepentant air. He was wearing the orange robes of his order but I detected more elaborate a garb hidden beneath.

"To what do I owe this undoubted pleasure, Brother Lanting?" he said, getting down to business; he motioned for me to take a seat upon the cushion provided. "You will excuse the rustic provisions, but we are a simple order, I hope you understand."

"Most certainly, Vertellen," I replied. "I think I understand only too well."

He didn't bat an eye—a cool one, this. From the first moment I had been conscious of his eyes, their unhidden contempt, how they'd been sizing me up, measuring me for combat. Such things too can be worked in reverse, for I could easily imagine him as the silken, quick-footed adept, more at home with rapier than broadsword, happier in shadow than in light.

"Your followers have desecrated and abused the hospitality of the Holy Order of Verinkad Knights," I said, coming straight to the point and allowing him no shades of grey. "Give reason why both you and your drunken followers should not be shown the gates of the city, and if necessary at the point of the sword."

He was silent for a moment, absorbing the full weight of my words, not rushing to his answers. When he did speak it was with the tone of the innocent holy man wronged. "You are filled with such anger, Brother Lanting; surely the celebrations of my goodmen brothers, men of simple pleasures, upon completion of such an arduous and pious trek, should engender less harsh appraisal. Should the faster now be decried when he breaks his fast?"

"Pious trek?" I repeated his words with some venom. "Your crusade has been naught but a pious pissup from day one. Understand me, Vertellen, I have had reports from the previous towns and cities you have visited upon this so-called crusade, and I know its nature only too well. I repeat my challenge; give your reason."

This time his answer was swifter and less reasoned. "Their coin is welcomed in the taverns and brothels from all that I hear. So far there are few complaints, except perhaps from some of your brethren who find their favourites otherwise engaged, and their place at the bar taken."

Despite myself, I felt the anger that I had so far managed to suppress rise to the surface. "I care not what you or your followers do within the confines of the taverns and brothels, nor do I really care if they collapse drunken upon the streets. What I do mind, however, is them entering waiting houses and then using them for illicit purpose."

"I understand your concerns," Vertellen accepted, "but you must see our problem; there just aren't enough rooms to house the number . . ."

"That is not reason," I snapped. "You will be given six hours with which to gather together your wayward flock. I will grant you leave to shelter one last night within these walls, but by midday tomorrow you will all have left Verinkad. I shall bid you good day." With this I had begun to leave, when his voice came one last time.

"That's right, your duty is done, holy man; you have made your city safe." His voice dripped sarcasm. "Go back to your broken stones, Brother Lanting," he called. "For all men are but broken stones; with them a strong man may build a wall, a wise man a bridge, a madman a temple."

He laughed!

I didn't look back.

*   *   *

A madman's temple; had that been my creation? It was a question I had to ask myself. The waiting houses, my gift to posterity, were now seemingly a tainted legacy. The vision had seemed so clear at the time, to bring the healing absolution of the gods to more of the people—the portable altars, the fragments from the temple—all now gone awry, evil men splashing tainted blood against the stone, drunken rabble fornicating before the altars.

As I entered the impressively large ancient well, that was the only entrance to the temple, I felt the situation to be grim indeed, for there was none of the usual lightening of the heart that generally occurred upon entering the holy of holies.

As I descended the spiral staircase around the wall of the well, the torches inset into the walls flickered, as if in tune with the god's agitation with their servant. At the halfway point of descent, I reached a place where part of the reinforced well-wall had been removed to gain entrance to the once hidden cavern beyond. Below, the spiralling stairwell twisted onwards into the gloomy depths, as the great city of Verinkad's ever more desperate search for fresh water drove it deeper.

Holding my torch out before me, I stepped into the temple of the most Holy Order of Verinkad Knights. The great cavern was hewn from the very stone; it contained over one hundred thick, sturdy columns, intricately chiselled with designs and letters from a language never yet deciphered, despite the best efforts of many a scholar. Standing within its great amphitheatre, I was as always left in awe by its dimensions. But on this occasion I felt there to be no time for breathing in the vastness of the temple, for the gods called to me, as certainly as if the cavern rang out with the sound of my name. I hurried forward, my light merely a firefly in the vast darkness of the crypt; here three great figures lay in stony repose, the original Verinkad Knights, a hundredfold the size of a normal man and laid out in all their ancient finery. How many millennia had they lain so, in their darkened grave, before they had been rediscovered a mere century before? A pinprick in time, for those who had been waiting for an eternity.

Here then was I, their keeper, their channel—such responsibility. I placed my torch within a holder, near the hand of one of the warriors, and watched as the warm glow spread across the stony fingers illuminating the cracks and fissures within the stone. Here part of a knuckle was missing, carried away to be used within the shrine of one of the waiting houses; here a piece of the hilt of the knight's sword, to a similar fate.

I looked closer, for I thought I detected more recent fractures. A process of decay had been in progress for millennia, but there was something sinister in this most recent series of fractures, as if an earthquake were silently shattering the old gods, breaking them out from beneath me—if they should crack apart then I too would fall. I studied the most minute hairline cracks with a new kind of desperation, as for the first time I accepted that in the short few days since I had last visited, the impossible had happened; the older cracks had noticeably opened, and new ones had spread in profusion where once smooth unbroken stone had ruled.

I had failed, I realized; I had allowed this desecration. But what could I do to save them? My gods—I held my head in my hands, in despair. What had I done?

(SMOKE AND MIRRORS)

III

VERTELLEN

AFTER LANTING'S DEPARTURE, I CALLED in Rivas and Caldar to inform them of the need to tie up loose ends more swiftly than I would have liked.

"Rivas," I said to the small rat-faced coin raker, "I want you to call upon those esteemed publicans of the good city of Verinkad, and impinge upon their time and graces for what we shall term a traditional donation to the holy trust. And Rivas, remember you are the emissary of a holy man, and as such carry much spiritual weight. I suggest you take this tack when dealing with the individual donors. You may also take a dozen of Caldar's men along, for their further instruction in these matters."

"Yes, Your Servitude." Rivas smirked and withdrew.

"You must have completed your tasks within three hours," I barked at his departing back. "Do not fail me!"

Now to Caldar; his hulking figure somehow shrank before me. "Now, Caldar my friend, what shall we do about you, eh?" His fear was palpable, yet he could crush me like a walnut within his hand. "You are my sword, Caldar, my champion. What could one such as you fear?" He didn't reply; perhaps he had reconsidered. "You will do as we planned. You will proceed, with the remainder of the men, and gather the coin of the followers . . ."

"No, master Vertellen." Caldar's voice was oddly high-pitched for a man of his build. "None of the others will enter those waiting houses—the spirits will get angry again."

"You are frightened of ghosts, Caldar. You who have killed with bare hands, afraid of mist and smoke?" I shook my head in mock disbelief, but it was no good; he was implacable in his aversion to those damn meditation rooms. And that, I knew in my heart, would be that, unless . . . A thought surfaced; the bonegrinder, the local spirit man, if I could enlist his services then perhaps the others could be convinced. Fools who could accept the presence of spirits could no doubt also be convinced of their removal, by an appropriately primitive ritual, or even better if he could be persuaded to provide some form of talisman, protective magics. I smiled to myself.

"Master . . . ?" Caldar said nervously, thinking perhaps that I had divined upon some form of punishment, but I was thinking only of some of those still bulging coin belts, and their drunken owners, lying unknowingly safe within Lanting's stony arms— for now!

* * *

The bonegrinder made his home in Tarnshuvil Alley. With Caldar and two others beside me, we reached this less than salubrious address in some ten minutes purposeful striding from the centre of Verinkad. That it was in the poorer quarter of the city was soon obvious. I decided to leave Caldar and the others outside, while I made first contact with the magic man. After a deal had been clinched, then they could be brought in to be dazzled by the bonegrinder's trickery.

The house itself seemed to be made out of a collection of broken masonry and shattered statuary, all cobbled together to the design of a madman. The lintel above the door bore the design of many hands, some dispensing seeds or holding varying forms of plant or herb. The doorway was an open invitation, but there were inscriptions chiselled into the stones that were obviously meant to be of far greater value than a door— protective runes. I chuckled to myself and crossed the threshold.

It was dark within, and it took a little time for my eyes to adjust to the lack of illumination. I was in a very large room, it seemed, with unidentified things hanging like animal pelts from rafters in the ceiling; the smell was oddly unsettling. I sidestepped several of these 'skins' and worked my way deeper into the room; there were other furs upon the floor but these seemed more recognisable. Deeper in, and more things to sidestep; this was turning into an obstacle course. These latest were large cocoon like bags hanging from ropes; there must have been at least a dozen of them. I approached the nearest one and lifted the flap that covered its top. I had to stand upon tiptoe to manage this, and jumped back with surprise, not so much at seeing a skull atop a pile of bones, but the simultaneous arrival of the bonegrinder's voice.

"You won't find me in there," he laughed, "or at least not yet."

I regained my composure and turned to face the voice. He had stepped through a curtain of black; silhouetted in light from beyond this curtain, he held a sinister aspect. I accepted his proffered invitation and stepped through the curtain into the lighted spaces beyond. Once again I had the task of readjusting my eyes to the change of light, as I observed the bonegrinder and his lair.

He was a tall black haired-man with a dark satanic beard, and wearing traditional black robes.

"Where is the fire?" I asked simply, glancing about in vain for the source of the light. There were shelves crammed full of jars and books, measuring devices, what appeared to be an embalming table, for it was the length of a very tall man, and sacks full of various herbs and other precious ingredients—but no fire. Neither was there any other source of light, no candles— for a moment I was nonplussed.

"Fire," the bonegrinder said, "is welcomed for its light and warmth, yet it is a friend I prefer at arms length."

Clever, I thought to myself, *smoke and mirrors*; Caldar and the others would be mighty impressed.

"What do you wish of me, Vertellen of the hard road?" he asked.

I sensed his distain.

"There are members of my party who, being of a superstitious nature, find ghosts in the most inopportune places. I would have their fears quelled by such simple protective talismans as you could provide."

"These ghosts," the bonegrinder muttered, seemingly disturbed at my request, "where are they?"

"Does it matter?" I replied. "My men claim their presence within Lanting's waiting houses."

"You are sure of this?"

"Look, there probably aren't any ghosts, "I said dismissively, "but my men are a superstitious lot; they jump at their own shadows. I just need to make them happy to return to the waiting houses."

"And why is that?" His eyes were glittering.

Suddenly I felt uncomfortable with the way things were progressing. "There are tasks they must perform there," I said, but his eyes were intense in their scrutiny.

I realized with some surprise that I was sweating—the heat from a hidden fire. I decided then and there to leave, scrap this plan of campaign and contemplate my losses in a more convivial setting.

"I bid you farewell, Bonegrinder," I said simply. "I fear we cannot be of the assistance to each other that I had first envisaged."

I was about to open the curtain and depart, when I heard the unmistakable sound of a sword being unsheathed, and Trevis's voice again, low in tone and dangerously close.

"Do not move a muscle, Vertellen, or I shall kill you and hang your flayed hide beyond the curtain, with your bones white and clean, pouched for posterity."

I froze.

"What will your men do in the waiting houses?" Again the questioning voice.

"They are cutpurses and thugs," I said, trying to keep my tone as light and unconcerned as I could manage. "I do not look to overtax their talents."

There was silence for a moment as if he was considering my words. "Murder in Verinkad," he said softly, so softly in fact that I was not sure it was directed at me. Nevertheless I answered.

"There is usually no need for killing," I assured him. "My men are professionals—of a kind. And I must warn you" I added, "I have half a dozen of them waiting outside, with orders to storm this place should I not return within the required time."

"You have three men," Trevis confirmed calmly, "and those I have just driven off with the Eye. I doubt they will return soon, or ever."

Startled by this latest turn of events, I was overcome with a strange malady that has rarely, if ever, struck me before—I was rendered speechless.

(ABSOLUTION AND REDEMPTION)

IV

KELDON

"THUS IT HAS COME TO me to be the chronicler of the fall, a position I never sought nor expected."

My drinking companion looks at me expectantly, so I continue.

"But one cannot speak of the fall without first speaking of blood, for whether it be the blood of the innocents, those murdered in the waiting houses or those of us in the Sortileger's Way, who afterwards fell upon the sword, it was to the crimson we were bound. Our pasts were soaked in the blood of others.

Upon this, the final night, we split up into groups and visited every waiting house we could find, slaying those within. It was ridiculously easy, most lay sleeping while only a few put up any worthwhile struggle. We daubed the stone fragments with their blood and fell in prayer before the altars, asking that our ghost burdens be lifted, and promising further sacrifice if we remained unaccepted.

We were barbarians at the gate, clamouring to be let into a fair city. We had only one last course of action open to us; the gates of paradise remained barred, so we bled our colleagues, and surrounded by the army of ghosts, we made at last for the temple of the Holy Order of Verinkad Knights."

I stopped for a moment, thinking of the past in wonderment and fear, and when I began again I was back in that cavern.

"There were only two dozen of us left now; we held our torches high and entered the temple. Ahead of us, an unguessable distance away, a single flame glowed in the darkness—the temple guard. Around me I felt the dead, like a tide of light breaking against the cold stones. As we moved forward a figure could be seen, silhouetted in red; it was a large man in the garb of the original Knights of Verinkad, a miniature version of the great godheads themselves—Brother Lanting!

At the sight of him, the dead quietened their wailing and a deathly silence filled the timeless crypt. He spoke then in a voice that echoed about us, as if it had come from the stones.

"Heed my words, haunted men. You will find no comfort here, no absolution."

"Stand aside, guardian," somebody replied, "or yourself join with the dead."

Weapons were brandished.

"The Verinkad Knights are breaking apart," he said simply. "They release the burden of a thousand evil and foolish men back into the world. Soon I will offer myself up as a receptacle; who else amongst you will accept redemption?"

There was uncertainty amongst the group.

"Accept the burden of the dead as your own," Lanting cried. "Atonement is at hand."

A cold wind began to pluck at our torches, swirling about us; the dead were within the wind, and its touch was the ice of eternity. My skin was growing colder now, as if I too were turning to stone.

Lanting began to step towards us, still calling for us to repent, and I became aware of another noise then, one that I hadn't noticed before, the sound of ice cracking, like some great egg breaking apart and letting loose a monstrous bird.

The tempo of the wind began to change, tearing at us now, ripping; within it the voices of the dead rose into a scream.

Suddenly from behind there came a greater light, and for a moment the whole temple lay illuminated, and the crumbling decaying forms of the stone knights were there for all to see— collapsing in upon themselves, turning to dust. One of us gave a strangled cry, and rushed forward to cast the proffered blood of our departed colleagues upon the nearest decaying giant, as if trying to extinguish a brushfire. It merely seemed to exacerbate the process, as the wind picked him up and cast him across the crypt to crash, broken-necked, against a stone column.

"You are fools," Lanting cried. "You understand nothing." And then he added, "who has brought the light?"

"I have," a new voice answered from our rear, and two new figures joined the tableau. One I recognized as the bonegrinder; the other I did not know, but he wore the robes of many we had slaughtered in the waiting houses.

The ghost wind tore our torches free, and lifted the smaller of us bodily into the air, spinning them about. The rest of us sought safety by falling to our stomachs, and clinging as tightly as possible to the stone pillars. Even from this position I could still see Lanting exhorting us, but I could also hear another voice; it must have been the bonegrinder.

"Lanting," he cried above the howling of the ghost wind, "what must we do?"

"The dead." Lanting replied. "Redeem yourselves, Trevis, Vertellen. Take their burden; if this should break free, Verinkad will be destroyed."

"This is madness." A new voice, this the one known as Vertellen. "We must get out of here, bonegrinder, while we still can."

The ghost wind tore several of my colleagues free of their precarious holds, and lifted them screaming into the dark. Being larger, I was proving more difficult to dislodge, but it could only be a matter of time, as the ghost wind formed itself into a whirlpool and grew ever more powerful in intensity.

Lanting now stood with his arms outstretched and his head raised. One of the whirlpools broke free from the main funnel and enveloped him. For a moment he was a ghost seen as if through mist, and then both he and the whirlpool were gone.

I had no time to contemplate his fate, as things were happening at a pace now. Firstly I was torn free from my hold upon one of the stone pylons, when struck by the bloodied body of one of the others, and felt myself being lifted roughly upwards.

Everything seemed to slow now, as if in the last moments of my life my mind was compensating for the shortage of time by stretching my perceptions to encompass the moment. I saw as if in a dream, or as a disembodied spirit looking down upon the world, the bonegrinder pushing the one called Vertellen forward, towards the funnel of the whirlpool, a sword against the other's chest. Somewhere there was light, though I could not see where. I was turned and twisted; the ghost wind playfully flung me against a column. My left arm was shattered in the impact, and then I was back in observation position again, spinning for a moment before I steadied. Beside me the bloodied body of another was also suspended, bobbing like a cork on a choppy sea. Below me I could hear Vertellen's voice, a combination of anger and fear, though I couldn't make out his words. The bonegrinder persisted in backing him up against the whirlpool, then lunged at him with the sword. In evading the thrust, he fell backwards into the whirlpool—it enveloped him as it had done Lanting, and a moment later he was gone.

I felt the power of the ghost wind lessening now, but it was still strong enough to hurl me across the temple, to crash violently against a far wall; a broken right shoulder now, to go with the arm. For the second time I had reason to thank my extra padding.

I was swirled back into the centre of the temple. I was slightly concussed now, and seeing the world through a grey haze, but I still saw the passing of the bonegrinder. He stepped, sword still in hand, and with what I could have sworn, even in my condition, was a half smile, into the whirlpool, and then he too was gone.

I was falling now, the ghost wind failing at last. As I crashed into stone for the third and last time, I felt the familiar cold touch of the dead, and saw in the dying of the light the vast shapes of the Verinkad Knights, renewed, towering beside me. I remembered no more.

*   *   *

Of course, if you ever go to Verinkad you may wish to visit the temple and see the three stone gods resting there within their vast chamber. And if you ever do, then you will know the story of how they came to be, and their names—Trevis, Lanting and Vertellen."

I smile wearily and move to finish my ale, but my new companion is looking at me in that way that I know only so well. How much of my tale he has heard I'm not sure. It always begins with the recognition, the widening of the eyes; when I see this I will move on.

Sometimes it is not so much fear but anger, like that bearded man in the tavern in Simora, who pushed aside an oaken table to get at me, and died moments later for his trouble; some such as he rush headlong to greet their deaths as would lovers, to embrace the cold steel to their hearts. Most, however, slink away as does my latest acquaintance, eyes aslant, puzzled, wondering as to the meaning of this haunting. Not that it is instantaneous; it may take several nights before the dead find me. Until then I am simply the traveller who has just arrived from elsewhere; I am always just arrived or just about to leave.

I have come to read the signs; as soon as there is hesitation, sudden breaking off of conversation, a questioning of already explained identity, then it is time to go. The dead will, of course, go with me; that much at least I will have achieved. An unrewarded exorcist am I, cursed to carry for all time the weight of other people's ghosts—Verinkad's price for my life, my redemption. I am to be the mirror of their dead. I curse them all!

The Bridge Across Forever

I

RAIN, LORD CORUM THOUGHT BITTERLY, this accursed land was a place without sun, without shadow, a place where a man, no matter how well protected, found himself damp—moisture seeped between armour plate and clothing—it affected the very psyche, men became inward looking, soldiers listless and weak, sickness abounded. Here things decayed, pavilions rotted, battles were endlessly prepared for but rarely fought, while leaders consulted oracles and other such conjure men. The Stealthlands, those in Serres had long ago named it, an accursed place where undesirables were often exiled, bastard royalty and troublesome religious orders.

Remembering something, Corum suddenly turned around in the saddle, sending a spray of half settled water off the hood of his dark cloak. "Tablis," he shouted back at the hunched figure plodding along behind him, a picture of rain—sodden misery, horse and rider alike.

The man looked up in some surprise. "Yes, my Lord," he said, attempting to raise some form of enthusiasm in his voice, but failing. A large man, his hood was thrown back to the rain, as if accepting the inevitable, and his short fair hair was plastered to his forehead. His large meaty hands gripped the reins limply.

"So how much further must we go before we are supposed to meet Tassik's men?"

"Not far my Lord," Tablis replied. "These woods soon give way to open field; the Burgarach knights have set up camps and a road block."

"A road block," Corum laughed, "without a road; truly we are in a land of madmen, Tablis."

Tablis, despite himself, almost smiled. "They are blocking all the tracks and paths now, my Lord, no matter how small."

Corum snorted. "They chase shadows, these men of Burgarach, and they think me a fool. I weary of their games, Tablis, and soon I will have proof of their deceit." He fell silent and they proceeded as before—only damper.

* * *

The camp of the knights of the holy order of Burgarach was a dismal sight, as seen through drizzle by the approaching riders— hastily erected pavilions and tents, roughly constructed stables wherein horses and soldiers alike could be seen sheltering, warming themselves against fitful fires that refused to light properly and gave off a black, noxious smoke. The shapes of soldiers could be discerned, moving between the various pavilions, running errands and carrying messages, their hurrying shapes accompanied by the splashing from fast-accumulating puddles. The path itself passed through the very midst of this encampment, and several large tree trunks had been laid rather unnecessarily across the path.

It took several moments, and not a few unsubtle threats from Corum, before any of the blank-eyed men huddling in their shelters would assist in the stabling of the horses. Thus fortified, his anger now standing out like the crest of a fighting cockerel, he stalked off towards the silver sun pennant, atop a distant and impressively large pavilion. The pennant flew at full mast, signifying to Corum's satisfaction that the Lord Tassik himself was in residence.

Tablis observed Corum's departure with a wry smile, and found himself within the smoke filled stables . . .

* * *

While Tablis was unfastening the saddles, and removing from the saddle bags the leather pouches that held their maps and documentation, a stable boy, his face blackened with soot from the constant fires, and with red and watery eyes, signalled for him to hold the horses still as he applied specially adapted blindfolds.

"The smoke," he murmured. "They rub their eyes against the posts."

Tablis nodded and thanked the lad with a silver piece. He now watched the grim faced men huddled around the fires— vests and tunics were dropped over posts inserted in the ground, seemingly specifically for that purpose. Body armour, breast plates and helms were propped close to the flames, so that the reflection glittered in their burnished surfaces, creating a myriad of flame casts—fire-spirits! Tablis felt himself becoming light in the head; *the smoke,* he thought, *it must be the smoke.* Red tendrils seemed to reach out for him. The stables were suddenly uncomfortably full of shadows, so he turned away to look out into the rain . . . A caravan, brightly decorated with mystic symbols, rolled into the encampment, and then as he stepped forward to be greeted by the cold touch of the rain, it was as if he had stepped through a curtain, and then it was gone again. *Just a mirage*, he thought, *such a vision brought upon by inhaling too much wood smoke.*

Squaring his shoulders, he marched off in the direction of the pavilion of Lord Tassik, his boots squelching in the mud.

*   *   *

Lord Corum stormed into the pavilion peeling off his sodden cloak, straightening his ruffles at the wrist and patting down his short black hair. A flunky, with an emblazoned silver rising sun upon a chemise blouse of gold, accepted his cloak, while another stepped through a dazzling curtain, depicting in one moment the great city of Serres, or as the holy order would have it, Burgarach, with its nine towers. Then as the curtain parted and re-formed, the great city was gone and the symbol of the rising silver sun had replaced it.

From beyond the curtain there came a familiar booming laugh, and he heard the Lord Tassik's voice, no doubt intentionally loud, informing his lackey to "bid the kingsman enter." Tassik used the word kingsman as another might announce the arrival of a bowel movement. Corum felt his face muscles contract, and he had to restrain his instincts to reach for the small curved blade dirk at his belt. In their last meeting, Tassik had referred to this weapon as highly decorative.

Even before the lackey could return, Corum had swept through the curtain and was making a stiff formal bow towards the gigantic figure, seated at the head of a long table. Lord Tassik had long, curly black hair and a ridiculously red beard, that reminded Corum of a badly fitted operatic prop. The sense of the ridiculous was further emphasised by Tassik's tendency for wearing his full body armour, probably in a misplaced attempt at affecting grandeur; it merely, to Corum's eye, painted him the buffoon he undoubtedly was—a puffed up toad of a man. The majority of the table was covered by sheeting, as if in a hurried attempt at concealment—maps and troop positioning, Corum surmised. The head of the table was stocked liberally with wine, and less so with knights of the holy order; besides Lord Tassik, only three of the other seats were taken. An elderly knight with greying hair and a vast beard, and two younger men who were so alike as to be identical twins, tall and clean shaven, glared at Corum with barely disguised malevolence. Gaily plumed helms were propped before them and occasionally patted like obedient dogs. The drumming of the rain upon the tenting was a constant if distant refrain.

"Corum," Tassik said smugly, "Goodman Corum, the hospitality of my house is always yours to enjoy. Pray be seated and join with us in saluting this, our joint enterprise, the scuppering of the false king Culthwarn, and therein closer ties between the crown and Burgarach."

Another lackey appeared and handed him a goblet of dark red wine, then motioned for him to take a seat next to the bearded warrior, and across from the young firebrands who continued to observe him with suspicion.

"Brother Clemis and brothers Brandis and Tanlin," Tassik said, indicating to them in turn. The old man grunted, and the two younger knights favoured him with the slightest of head tilts.

"Your trip to Costanza was productive, I hope?" Tassik's voice hinted at some prior knowledge of the situation.

"There has been a vanishing," Corum confirmed, "twelve men, all young and healthy, handy with the bow, one and all."

"So the crusade reaches Costanza." Tassik gave a glance to Clemis, who stroked his beard thoughtfully and spoke up. "We have further reports from our patrols in the south; the crusade passed through there some months ago, up to a hundred men from a dozen villages, and always the same story. The king, they say, rode in with a vast hoard of followers, great clashing of cymbals and horns bellowing, men in armour upon horseback and lines of ordinary peasants with longbow and sword following behind. "The Crusade," they called. "Come and join the Crusade, for the king!"

"And a nameless king at that," Tassik muttered, interrupting him.

"Aye," one of the younger knights agreed, "but we know his name; it is the bastard spawn of the one who once called himself the great protector." He turned and spat with some venom, and a great deal of accuracy, into a spittoon set back from the table.

Corum lowered the goblet, aware of the sudden drop in room temperature.

"You must excuse my brother his manners," Tassik said at length. "We of Burgarach no longer have the benefit of the royal assent, and so are forced to make do as best we can in this backwater." He smiled, "I'm sure you understand our position."

Corum nodded in return. "The passing of the age is always the last song to be heard in the lands," he intoned solemnly and sipped his wine, the faintest hint of a smile beginning to form.

At this moment a lackey scuttled up to Tassik, and relayed something in hushed tones that made the Burgarach knight nod and clap his hands, a gesture obviously meant to indicate the meetings end.

"Your liege has arrived, and I have had a room prepared for you. I hope you inform your king of the hospitable nature of the knights of Burgarach." With that and a slight tilt of the head he was gone, his knights trailing after him.

Corum toasted their backs with some ceremony, wondering to himself suspiciously what had come up to make them depart in such a rush. Having found himself momentarily alone, Corum hurried over to the table and lifted a corner of the coverings. He had already guessed what would be there, extremely extensive maps, although from the portion he could see, he was unable to make out if they were of areas close to the great city of Serres. Perhaps if he could see more; he began to turn back the cover to reveal the greater part of the still hidden cartography. But at that moment a lackey entered the room, and Corum let the cover drop back into place with practised nonchalance. "Very interesting," he said, smiling, "but without the Lord Tassik to explain it to me, I'm afraid I can't make head or tail of these contingencies. Perhaps, my good man, you are sent to enlighten me?"

"You are to follow me," the lackey said simply.

"Am I now?" Corum said, raising his eyebrows. He drained the last of his wine and followed the lackey, who led him to an annexe off the main pavilion. Here a hot bath had been poured and simple robes lain across a comfortable looking bed. Tablis was waiting for him, looking dishevelled but uncomplaining as always.

"Tassik was his usual charming self," Corum admitted. "His words are like blows delivered with a velvet covered cosh. He knows I suspect him, and fears what I represent, but he dares not turn upon me, not just yet; his plans are not sufficiently advanced—his very caution betrays him. Think on it, Tablis my friend," Corum continued, "we have mass recruiting of peasants for some mythical king . . ."

"Culthwarn is no myth," Tablis interrupted. "He was banished here in . . ."

"No, no . . ." Corum waved him silent. "Culthwarn was merely a shadow, a stalking horse. He was a weak individual, personally spineless and of no danger; unfortunately the regent ignored such representations, both from myself and others, and banished him." He was silent for a moment, as if considering implications, and not for the first time Tablis imagined a small cross being added to some hidden interior check list. *If enough crosses were added*, Tablis thought to himself, but he left the implied question unanswered; the title Kingmaker was one Corum secretly coveted, he felt sure. Perhaps the king's choice of Corum for this mission was more to do with getting him as far away as possible, as any real desire to uncover plots of the Burgarach knights.

"Mass vanishings," Corum said at last. "Where are all the armies, eh? What has happened to them?"

"My visions give no clear answer, my Lord," Tablis admitted, "but there have been such happenings elsewhere, though on a much smaller scale. In Halleck they place boy children in red-white coffins, gaily decorated with the faces of their gods, and parade them upright, upon litters, invoking the spirits to choose their sacrifice from amongst those offered. Always one of the coffins returns empty—a vanishing; the gods are satisfied for another year."

"It is all just priestly trickery,"Corum scoffed. "The coffin is false sided, and they either kill the child or sell it to the slave trade."

"Barbarians," agreed Tablis. "But there is something of the vanishing parade about this, wouldn't you say? A certain similarity?"

"Then where is the false side?" Corum said in exasperation. "A hidden place where hundreds of men may disappear to without trace. No, my friend, the Burgarach knights are gathering together an army. Tassik invents bastard kings to fool the unwary, and then compounds the deceit by pretending to

scour the countryside for this nonexistent man and his followers."
Corum was now pacing up and down in agitation. "Yet in doing
so, who then has patrols of his men spread out far and wide?
Who then has access to the very villages he pretends to protect?
I am but one man, Tablis; I do not monitor the movements of
his knights, but I fear that patrols that start out with twelve men
suddenly become twenty-four and then forty—who is to tell?
In such ways large numbers of men may be gathered almost
imperceptibly, and kept upon the march, only to be brought
together when the time is ripe."

"And yet, my Lord," Tablis reminded him, "the tales we
have heard from the villagers tell of a great king and his vast
following, of blaring horns, of banners and battle horses—not
small unheralded patrols."

"But can we believe them?" Corum protested. "Tassik's men
must have put the fear of reprisal upon these simple peasants;
they are given the same story to tell, and repeat it parrot fashion."

"That would explain the similarity in their descriptions,"
Tablis admitted, although his tone remained sceptical.

Corum rubbed a weary hand through his dark hair, suddenly
feeling very tired. "You must understand, Tablis, "he said at last,
"I search always for answers I may grasp. Tassik and his like
I can understand; what you deal in . . ." He didn't finish, but
Tablis well understood his difficulty; if some form of magical
enchantment was involved in these disappearances then Corum
would be out of his territory. No diplomatic move or elegantly
sinister threat would be of use here—confrontation without
sword, something they both specialized in, each in his own way.

"They have provided you with suitable accommodation, I
trust?" Corum said at last.

Tablis nodded. "Simple but comfortable, my Lord." A spot
in the stables, in point of fact, but for the moment he chose not
to reveal this calculated insult; there would be time enough later,
besides there was something about the wood smoke that seemed
to initiate his visions—it might yet prove a profitable turn of
events.

Taking his leave of Corum, he exited the pavilion of Lord Tassik and began the muddied trek back towards the stables. The rain had lightened somewhat, little more now than a heavy mist settling over the camp. The first thing he noticed was that the standard above the pavilion was now flying at three-quarters, signifying the Lord's absence. The second, and more interesting, was the presence of the deep wheel ruts cut into the muddied earth, not long departed if he was any sort of judge. One or perhaps more than one caravan had been, albeit briefly, within the encampment—there had been no such wheel ruts when he had traversed the same ground earlier. He remembered his vision!

Bending down for a moment, as if adjusting his boots, Tablis clicked his fingers and smiled at the thing that appeared between his beefy hands. It hovered there for a moment—delicate and small. *Dance for me,* he thought, *dance . . .*

It began to move; there was a rattling noise, like the subtle desecration of a grave.

"Follow," he whispered, and there was a localized wind—the mist . . .

Tablis turned and headed back towards the stables, a large man, shoulders hunched, arms hanging slack at his side, a picture of misery.

II

A SLATE GREY DAWN AND an evil blustery wind, such were the gifts provided. Lord Corum observed the figure of Tablis as he led out the horses; he seemed preoccupied with the paddock across which he was walking, as if searching its churned up surface for some unnamed sign. He finally arrived at Corum's side, and speaking in little more than a whisper he said. "There have been movements overnight."

"How do you mean?" Corum replied, lowering his voice to match that of his liege.

"You see these churned up patches? Many men on horseback; the stables have almost emptied."

"The Crusade at work, eh, Tablis?"

The big man shrugged. "Possibly, my Lord," he said, "but several at least wait within the woods to follow our progress."

"Spies," Corum spluttered, and despite himself his voice rose dangerously high. "How long has this been happening, Tablis?"

"Ever since our arrival, my Lord; I broach it with you now only because I expect this part of our investigation better carried out in secret."

"You're damn right."

"In that case," Tablis said "we shall have need of a diversion."

*   *   *

For Corum it had all begun with a letter and a name, Tablis—the Lord Prendaguard's favourite. It wasn't usually Corum's practice to accept stray astrologers or fake conjure men as companions, yet Prendaguard himself was a favourite of the king and refusal might have been seen as unwise. Part of the letter had spoken of Tablis's talents for visions and the invoking of ancient magic.

"He shall travel as your liege," the missive had boldly stated, "a disguise that I believe amuses him?"

Amusement! Lord Corum thought about the uncomplaining Tablis, who was at this moment working some infernal conjure upon the path in front of them; it was not an emotion readily associated with the big man. To Corum, Tablis seemed to be a man without artifice or bluster, a stolid farmer in a field of wonders.

While lost in these considerations, Corum hadn't noticed a sudden movement in the woods to their left; a group of three men leading their horses suddenly emerged into the daylight— Tassik's spies! They appeared to be preparing to tail some unseen companion of Tablis or Corum, for they gave neither man even the briefest of glances, passing Corum within touching distance and looking straight ahead, with the occasional glance downwards as if tracking phantom hoof prints appearing in the muddied path. Corum held his breath until they had passed him by, as if frightened his slightest movement might break whatever enchantment Tablis had placed upon them.

"What fey dream beguiles them?" he asked at last, as the big man returned to his horse.

"Smoke ghosts, my Lord." Tablis smiled, but would not elaborate further.

"How long will they remain like that," Corum asked, "following shadows?"

Tablis shrugged. "I'm not sure," he admitted, "but hopefully long enough for our purposes."

"And what might they be?" Corum said, looking at Tablis with an evaluating stare.

Tablis seemed to accept this readily enough; he understood as well as Corum the changing status of their relationship. The time for diplomacy was past; now was the time for the conjure man to cast aside the robes of servitude, for more elaborate a garb.

"My Lord, while in the encampment I had cause to notice the presence of wheel ruts made by a caravan. It was to this caravan that several of my visions pertained."

Corum nodded. "Yet what has this to do with the so-called vanishings?"

"I believe that Tassik is being assisted in his plans by a man of power."

"Another conjure man,"Corum groaned.

Tablis smiled. "I'm afraid so, my Lord."

"Then why have we not seen these wheel ruts in the paths we have traversed over the past few weeks?"

"For the same reason those spies walked by us without seeing; their attention was diverted—as has been ours."

"By magic?" Corum asked uncertainly. He felt odd even discussing such a thing.

Tablis just nodded, and directed Corum's attention to the spot upon the path where he had been kneeling moments before. A wheel rut was now visible, and as they watched it extended itself out along the track.

"The mist before our eyes lifts" Tablis intoned.

"Then let us follow," Corum said. "Lead the way, Tablis."

*   *   *

"Lord Tassik of the Holy Order of Burgarach Knights . . ." the herald announced, and Tassik dismounted. Behind him forty men in full armour massed their horses and checked their weapons.

The small figure greeted Tassik with its usual furtiveness; once, in a less restrained moment, Tassik had clapped the small man upon the shoulder, the force of which had threatened to drive him into the muddied ground like a rotted post. Trackerman the conjure man; his dark hair stood out like burnt bristles, while his robes, black as the night, contained hidden riddles. Tassik never looked too closely; there were shadows closeted within, things he wished not to discover. Touching him had been like brushing up against something cold and damp; beyond that first occasion he had never done it again. Trackerman was the Stealthlands, Tassik thought, the very embodiment; something within him had died and yet, cloaked in fey power, had willed itself to go on.

"Bring me the tapestries, magic man," Tassik ordered. "I must see them anew."

Trackerman bowed his head slightly. "As you command, my Lord."

The small figure scurried back to the caravan, which awaited him in the very centre of the field.

Now even more of Tassik's knights were massing; they neared a hundred. Amongst them was Brother Brandis, who organized them into lines of four riders abreast. Lances and swords were being hefted into position; helms were being placed upon heads. The grizzled face of Clemis appeared at his leader's side. "All is in readiness, my Lord."

"The full complement has arrived?"

Clemis nodded. "All are gathered here with the exception of Tanlin and his men, who continue to watch for the movements of the Kingsman Corum."

"And how has our young firebrand taken it?"

"Not well I'm afraid, my Lord; he is crushed at missing out upon our moment of glory and revenge. The brothers tossed a coin and it was Tanlin who lost."

"He will be with us in spirit at least." Tassik understood well the young man's grief. "I have waited so long for this moment, Clemis, all these years in this place, the waiting, the planning and now the moment . . ."

"Trackerman returns with the tapestries," Clemis said, interrupting his master's reverie.

"Ah yes the tapestries; oh glorious magic."

Trackerman drove a post into the soft earth and began to unfurl a long and intricate tapestry depicting in turn, woods and fields, within which groups of men stood or sat, holding bow and sword, peasants mainly, though amongst them were those dressed as Burgarach knights. The tapestry came to its end at another post, which was driven solidly into the wet earth. An assistant stepped forward and handed Trackerman the next tapestry which continued where the last had finished. It showed more of the assemblage area, more men and horses, knights leaning upon swords staring out as if watching for the arrival of others. Amongst them were faces Tassik recognized. The magic of the tapestries never failed to entrance him; with each viewing they changed, as more and more of his forces passed into the setting. They appeared in due course upon the other side, steadily filling up the initially empty fields.

A third tapestry was erected, and then a fourth.

Tassik continued to look at the faces of the men; it was as if he were looking in a two-way mirror, watching them as they observed him. An army prepared in stealth—he smiled to himself in triumph.

He remembered Trackerman's muddled ramblings, when he had first come to him with the tapestries. He had thought the conjure man mad, until the first experiments; those first frightened, uncomprehending peasants looking out at him, and then he'd understood the magnitude of the opportunity.

A bridge, Trackerman had called it, a bridge across forever. Using such a bridge an army might traverse vast stretches of countryside without facing fatigue, enemies or starvation; they might actually appear under their enemy's very noses. He smiled again, walking to the fourth of the tapestries; this one differed from its fellows in that it depicted the lands adjoining the assemblage area; they stretched away into the middle distance. The spires of the great city glinted in the afternoon sun—he felt a familiar thrill. Time upon that side of the tapestry seemed to move much slower than upon his. In all the months that had encompassed the first tentative passage of those original peasants, to the mass movement of men and horses that had followed, he had calculated by the adjusting shadow casts, taken less than four hours tapestry time, as he had come to think of it. It would give the Kingsmen no time to react; his element of surprise would be total, and victory was assured.

Lord Tassik left his contemplation and returned to his horse. "It's time!" he said to the sinister figure of Trackerman. "We go in now."

Trackerman nodded. "As you wish, my Lord. All is in readiness."

"And you?"

Trackerman smiled. "I shall follow your Lordship."

"You don't want to miss the culmination of our endeavours, do you?"

"Certainly not, my Lord," Trackerman said.

Tassik placed the helm upon his head. "Clemis," he bellowed.

"Yes, my lord."

"Move them out."

The first line of mounted Burgarach knights approached the first tapestry, and as they breasted it the horses threw their heads but continued walking none the less, vanishing into the tapestry as into mist. A second line followed, and soon tapestries two and three were being similarly approached. Lord Tassik watched it all with a growing pride.

Trackerman also watched, but whatever thoughts he entertained he gave no hint.

III

—————

By the time Tablis and Corum arrived at the field, following the no longer invisible wheel ruts, the vast majority of Burgarach knights had already gone and the last dozen or so were just departing, amongst them Tassik himself. Seeing them he laughed in triumph. "Too late, kingsman. The crusade has begun." With this he called out to the magic man. "Hold them off until all of us are through, Trackerman, and then destroy the tapestries behind you."

Trackerman nodded. His dark robes whipped about him as if a wind were coming from within—there was the stink of decay.

Corum jumped off his horse and drawing his dagger was about to rush forward to engage the figure in black when Tablis's voice rose in warning to dissuade him. "No, my Lord. He is death. Your dagger will have no effect." The big man was suddenly at his side. "This battle is mine."

Tablis's hands moved in a series of complex passes. "Return," he commanded. "Dance for me."

Something began to form in the space between his moving hands—a mist; it began to coalesce. Something dark and fetid struggled to become free; mist entwined it, entrapped it. Tablis's hands began to move again, a master puppeteer pulling invisible strings. The mist cage began to turn ever swifter, folding, inwards then out, it grew in size—things were struggling to escape.

Corum looked away from the cage for a moment and saw that the dark form of Trackerman was closing the distance between them, walking as if through treacle. His robes rustled in unfelt wind; somewhere within there were lights—green, red, and gold, lights—winking, growing in size. Corum felt as if he were falling into that darkness, being drawn inwards: he could see the army, in there, waiting. The red sparks were men in glinting, burnished battle armour, the green the battle standards flying proudly, and amidst it all the golden king calling out to him, calling . . .

A hand struck him across the face. Blood began to trickle from his nose.

"I'm sorry, my Lord, but you mustn't look into the lights."

Tablis, Corum thought, in his blurry state of mind, *the crusade . . .* Shaking his head, he looked back into the cage. It had caught fire now; fiery hands tried to reach out for them through restraining mist. It was spinning so swiftly now that the growing detail was hard to make out.

Trackerman had almost reached them when something within him broke at last; he exploded! Shattered bone and decaying, putrefying flesh were scattered across the field. Released, the black robes hung in the air for a moment, flapping as if a gigantic bat, and then they collapsed—the lights fleeing for the tapestries—green, red, and gold. They disappeared within, setting the tapestries alight behind them.

The cage had stopped spinning now; whatever was inside had ceased to struggle.

"What happened?" Corum asked simply.

"The magic man was little more than another disguise," Tablis said. "I just stripped it clean, layer by layer, until the thing inside was forced to flee."

"So what's in the cage of mist?"

"Fragments, my Lord" Tablis said. "A dozen desecrations against those already dead."

"Are they at peace now?"

"Yes, my Lord, their dance is over."

"And the crusade . . . ?"

"I'm afraid Tassik was right; it appears we are too late."

The cage of mist had decayed and now drifted across the field, mingling with the smoke from the burning tapestries.

"What madness is this?" Corum muttered, seeing beneath the flames the gathered army.

"We have found the hidden armies." Tablis replied. "They have, via Trackerman's magic, entered another place."

"They go to attack Serres." Corum roared in sudden understanding, seeing at last the final tapestry with its towers and spires glinting in the afternoon sun—red flames licked at its edges, a blackness.

"They must be warned," Corum said in desperation. "The city will be taken." With this he braced himself and stepped into the still burning tapestry.

"No, my Lord," Tablis called in warning. But it was already too late; Corum had vanished.

Tablis, faced with an almost instantaneous choice, followed him through the flames and into the tapestry.

*   *   *

They found themselves in an empty field, sodden and badly cut up from the passage of feet, both human and equine, not unlike the one they had just left.

"We are too late," Corum groaned. "They will have begun their assault upon the city."

Tablis just shook his head and knelt down to observe more closely the field's surface. "I think not, my Lord."

"How do you mean?" Corum joined the big man, who was pointing to a group of footprints intermingled with the occasional hoof mark.

"All headed north," Tablis noted, "but they are of varying ages."

"I don't understand." Corum scratched his head. "In the tapestries they were all gathered together."

"Exactly," Tablis agreed. "The tapestries lied; once again the magic of disguise."

"So the city . . ." Corum began, trying to understand the magic man's point, "the city first came under attack much earlier?"

"I don't believe so, my Lord. In fact, I don't believe that this is the city of Serres at all."

They stood looking at the distant spires glinting in the sunlight.

"I'm afraid I must disagree with you, Tablis my friend. I would know the city of Serres anywhere—those spires."

"Enchantment," Tablis said. "I'll show you my Lord." He took from his pocket a small stone. "The Eye of Truth," he said. Sanded down upon one side, so as to be perfectly flat, its interior was a clear crystal except for flecks of gold.

Corum placed this against one eye and closed the other. He found himself in sudden darkness.

"What the Abyss?" He pulled it away and the field and its surrounds returned. "What of this, Tablis? What queer magic is at work?"

"I'm not sure, my Lord," Tablis admitted, "but one thing I am certain about is that we are not in the vicinity of the great city of Serres. In fact, I would be tempted to say we are no longer in the lands at all."

Corum handed the stone back. "I don't think I understand."

"We're still in the tapestry," Tablis said, "or at least I think we are."

"But the tapestry burned?"

"The part that protruded burned, my Lord, but that was merely the doorway; we are now inside."

"Inside . . . ?" Corum grumbled, irritated at Tablis's evasiveness. "Inside what?

"A clever box, a wizard's magic device—entrapped."

"Trackerman," Corum said, in sudden understanding, and Tablis nodded.

"The magical caravan; I saw it in my visions but I never realized its true nature. To maintain a clever box of that size . . ." He shook his head.

"But if what you say is correct then we have been duped, all of us, Tassik and his men too."

Tablis smiled, but it wasn't a comforting effort. "I fear you speak the truth, my Lord."

"So what should we do? Follow the men of Burgarach into whatever Trackerman has prepared for them, or try to find a way out of this clever box, as you term it—Trackerman's caravan?"

"I fear, my Lord, that the only way out is to confront the magic that called itself Trackerman and try to best it."

"Those lights . . . ?" Corum said, and Tablis nodded.

"It attempted to destroy the entrance behind it, so there was certain deference to my powers."

"And do you think you can best it again?"

"I hope to do so, my Lord, but it will be stronger here within its own construction. First we must dispense with this enchantment for good, or we will struggle to come to grips with our enemy." He placed the stone against his eye and muttered unhappily, "This darkness is a problem; later we will need illumination."

He handed the stone to Corum. "Hold it as before and under no circumstances release it. It will be your link with our true situation; remember, my Lord, whatever you might see, we are in a box, a potentially very large one, but a box nonetheless. Whatever the Trackerman spirit has collected in here it resides, lost in the darkness; this enchantment is merely a spell for the Burgarach knights, one we should do our best to ignore."

Corum nodded. "I heed your words of counsel, Tablis, yet how do you propose to illuminate darkness? I can only see with the aid of this stone."

Tablis smiled. "I'm afraid I don't, my Lord, at least not yet; it would give away our position."

"You mean we are going to stumble through the darkness like a couple of blind men, ignoring all the while the lighted path."

Tablis laughed. "Yes, my Lord, that's about the strength of it."

"Yet you can provide illumination when the need arrives?"

"I can and will," Tablis assured him, "yet for now we must make do with the Eye."

Corum sighed, closed his left eye and pressed the stone up against his right. He felt Tablis's large hand grasp his shoulder. In the newly rediscovered darkness the big man's voice was at his ear. "Lead the way, my Lord," he said, "and watch out for the lights."

*   *   *

Corum fell over something in the darkness and went crashing down; Tablis stumbled after him. Corum hung onto the stone as if his life depended upon it; he did, however, open his eyes momentarily. They were scrambling to pick themselves up after tripping over a stone marker. They were upon the edge of a road. *No*, Corum thought as he closed his eyes again, *back into darkness.*

"What was it we tripped over?" he asked Tablis, aware of the big man kneeling beside him.

"It seems to be the body of a horse," Tablis replied, "or at least the skeleton." He moved his hands over the darker patch in the gloom.

"How long has it been here then?"

"Hard to tell," Tablis said.

Corum, having replaced the stone to his eye, noticed a spark of light, moving in the blackness. "Are you using illumination, Tablis?" he asked.

"No," Tablis replied, drawing close to him, the skeleton suddenly forgotten. "What do you see?"

"A spark of light, very faint, possibly distant. No, now it's gone again."

"Inform me immediately should you see it return, my Lord," Tablis advised him. "Now, let us continue."

Corum held the stone tightly to his eye, and with Tablis holding onto his shoulder began once again. Despite himself, an afterimage of the road remained and he imagined them slowly shuffling along it towards the distant city, its spires still gleaming.

*   *   *

Tassik led the charge against those defenders who had raised a makeshift bulkhead at the shattered gates. Already the fields were red with the blood of the fallen, mostly kingsmen felled by the sword and axe. Archers fired upon them from above, yet they had already breached the walls once; soon the defenders would be swamped by sheer numbers. Fires were being lit upon the walls now; screaming rent the air.

Clemis was suddenly beside him in the carnage.

"The city walls burn," Tassik laughed in triumph. "Soon our standard shall fly atop its towers." He felt strangely light-headed; an acrid smoke drifted across the field of battle.

Clemis seemed oddly detached, staring at him as if seeing him for the first time. Tassik became aware of the sound of clashing armour, the blowing of horns. All about him the battle raged, but he was aware of a change; amongst the battle standards of Burgarach now were other standards—vermilion fire upon a green background. Amongst his men were now the helms of others, golden helms. "Clemis," he cried. "To me, Clemis, to me!" But the old soldier was turning his horse away, rallying towards the golden king who rode now into the flames and battle, surrounded upon all sides by his standards, flapping proudly in the breeze.

Tassik felt a madness gripping him, as for a moment he too was tempted to rally to the side of the king, the unnamed golden king, but then a deeper, stronger power gripped him, as he remembered what he was.

"To me," he screamed to any who would listen, and urged his horse forward into the fray, swinging his sword wildly.

*   *   *

The light had returned; Corum was certain of that now, a red fire in the darkness. He hadn't been sure, at first; that's why he hadn't informed Tablis. But now he was sure and yet he still didn't speak of it—a part of him sensed that Tablis had been using him, forcing him to stumble through this darkness without illumination. The more he thought about it the angrier he became. Here was a light in front of him, just waiting for him to reach out and grasp it, yet Tablis was like an anchor, weighing him down with his malign presence.

A thought began to crystallize; what if he should turn and push the conjure man away, smash him, knock him down and then flee from him? With the stone in his possession, and then the light, it would be he and not Tablis who would wield the power.

Corum smiled to himself in the darkness, holding the stone to his eye, watching the fire spirit dance.

* * *

The blow knocked Tablis sideways, sent him spinning. "Corum," he shouted.

There was the sound of someone running somewhere ahead of him—Corum was fleeing, but why?

The lights, Tablis realized, *the lights had returned— Trackerman's fire-spirits.* He cursed his choice of Corum for carrying the Eye, and tried to follow the receding noises, but in the total darkness his instincts were not to run blindly, but to creep forward. For a moment he was tempted to open his eyes, but he knew that to be pointless; better the utter neutrality of the darkness than the actively deceitful world of the enchantments.

He stopped to listen more closely, and then he could hear something; it sounded like distant muffled screams. Had Corum been taken by Trackerman's lights? Or perhaps it was Tassik's men. Whichever, he was left with little choice. The time had come to announce his presence.

Sitting upon the cool smooth surface that was the base of the clever box, still without opening his eyes, Tablis removed from his robes a small collection of bones. He placed them out in front of him in order, brushing his fingers across them in turn. "Dance," he called softly. Coldness began to infect his fingers; he sensed rather than saw the mist forming—there was a localized wind.

"Fire," he said, and saw it in his minds-eye, a red fire-brand, hovering in front of him. Keeping his eyes closed, he rose to his feet and began to follow it.

*   *   *

Corum had reached the light; he was almost upon it, reaching out for it with his left hand, when it darted away so swiftly that he toppled over something in surprise. His clutching hand was empty, and his mind racing at the sight, brief though it was, of white bones gleaming eerily in the glow. He was angry now, and frightened. The glowing light hovered nearby.

Keeping the stone pressed firmly to his eye, he got to his feet and started after it again; still it retreated, leading him through the blackness, until vanishing at last, as if tiring of the game. He noticed now, for the first time, that there were other lights glowing all about him, like distant army encampments. He marched off towards the nearest one, taking giant steps, yet it came no closer, seeming to dance away from him. He dashed towards another, a golden orb, but it too evaded him, rising high into the air, then accelerating away. He chased it frantically for a time, falling over things in his haste, blackened things. He paid no heed, for he wished only to possess that light—the golden light.

*   *   *

Thrown from his horse, Tassik reached the walls at last; about him the new warriors in red and gold were swarming upon his men. Swinging his sword, he carved a path through them; they parted as if smoke ghosts. He crashed into the wall itself—it exploded. A dark shape loomed up in front of him, like a corpse rising out of its grave. He turned away—head down, running now, brushing aside with flailing sword-arm the things that attempted to cling to him, ghostly hands. He burst through a fetid wall. Things cascaded down upon him, broken things—he ran on.

A pulsating green light hovered nearby and as he stumbled towards it he saw something moving within. He gagged! There was a taste of ash in his mouth. Green lantern, golden orb, red flame—fire consuming flesh into green corpse light. He was falling through a grey nightmare, stumbling over bodies, crushing bone to dust.

A fire-spirit came for him now, dropping from the vaulted darkness above like a scarlet spider upon a dropline of fine spun gold. For a moment he was trapped, held in webs of fire wrapping about his arms and legs, gathering to the sword like a wavering sickly aura. But it was quickly broken, torn apart by his skeletal hand, its white bones glinting in the flame. He would have screamed if he could, but the fire had taken his tongue.

*   *   *

Corum fell sprawling over someone in the darkness; another figure crashed up against him. The stone was dislodged from his hand. He opened his eyes; he was in the midst of a battle field. All about him the Burgarach knights were under attack by warriors in red and gold. He closed his eyes again and got down upon his hands and knees, feeling about in the ancient ash for the stone. His searching fingers discovered bones and more bones.

Somebody else tumbled over him; a sword clattered next to him and he grasped after it. His fingers found not the blade but the stone. He hesitated, placing it against his eye once more, frightened now at what it might reveal—the temptation was too great. There were fire-spirits all about him, attacking the dimly visible shapes of men—swords against magic.

He tried to back away, but noticed a fire-spirit coming for him. Yet it seemed different, somehow warmer, more diffuse.

"Corum," he heard someone call after him, "stay close to the light."

"Tablis . . . ?"

"Yes, my Lord."

"By the Abyss I'm sorry, my friend. I was overcome by madness."

"Later, my Lord. First I must do what I can to save Tassik's men."

Corum sensed Tablis's presence. A localized wind appeared to gather around them; there was the sound like a clicking of bones.

"Dance," he heard Tablis whisper.

Bones, all about them, rising from the ash, joining together, skeletal forms. They began to move against the fire-spirits, and Corum noticed for the first time that many carried swords and were swinging them like scythes.

The battle of magics was joined, the fire-spirits at their eyes, yet no longer blinding, plucking uselessly at empty sockets. A green lantern was gutted, spilling out putrid liquid and its corpse light dissipating; another, this time the skeleton was set alight by the fire-spirits and gave off smoke, but still it continued to cut and slash. The fire-spirits too began to be carved asunder, their fragments scattered and broken. Rising above all the slaughter and destruction was the golden orb that had enchanted him before.

They stood silhouetted in the warm light of Tablis's magic fire-brand, yet to Corum they suddenly seemed pathetically small figures, childlike and fragile, easily crushed. Despite these fears, Tablis's army of skeletons were steadily destroying the Trackerman spirit's servants.

The golden orb now began to pulsate, slowly at first and then faster, drawing together the remainder of its servants, undamaged by Tablis's assaults. It began to change, attempting to attain true form. Even as Corum watched, the various segments began to alter, green lanterns becoming hard carapace scales, burnished and glowing, fire-spirits vestal wings that slowly began to expand and unfurl. The golden orb divided into four ancient all-seeing eyes. Corum stood watching in wonder and awe. It began to glow from within, so brightly that Corum had to turn his head away, and when he turned back it was gone. Only a small amber casting remained, glowing faintly within the vast chamber. The sound of a mighty thunderclap came from somewhere far away.

"The clever box has been opened!" Tablis called out in triumph.

His skeletal soldiers were collapsing back into the ash, while amongst them the dazed survivors of Tassik's army milled about in confusion. A face loomed up at him out of the gloom, bearded and craggy.

"Clemis," he called, but the old soldier pushed him aside as if he were still lost in some grey fog. Tablis made his way to where the casting lay and soon it had vanished into his pockets.

"What now?" Corum asked, still holding the stone to his eye.

"There's no longer any need for that, my Lord," Tablis informed him. "The enchantment went when the box was opened."

Corum opened his eyes and the scene remained the same— Tablis with his magical fire-brand floating before him, and around them the remains of Tassik's army.

"We had best get out while we can; now that the magical seal has been broken the clever box will begin to collapse."

"And Tassik's men . . . ?" Corum probed.

"They should follow us if they are able," Tablis replied.

"I saw Clemis a moment before," Corum informed him.

"Good, then they will have somebody they can trust to follow."

"Yet he remains lost as if in a trance."

"Not for long," Tablis assured him.

*   *   *

In single file they approached the light-filled opening, which they seemed to have been marching towards for hours. At first the doorway had seemed vastly distant and yet immense; now as they edged closer its size decreased. It was as if they were in a house that shrunk about them as they moved towards the door—the clever boxes collapse was quickening.

"Will we make it in time?" Corum wondered aloud, and Tablis, who led the band of survivors, thirty or so, laughed.

"I hope so, my Lord," he said. "Being crushed to death inside a collapsing clever box is not an end I would like to recommend."

By the time they reached the doorway itself, it was barely thrice the size of a normal door, and by the time all the Burgarach knights, still within trance and following Tablis's magic fire-brand, had been ushered through, it was twice as small again. The collapse was on in earnest now.

Corum had to bend over in his leap through, while Tablis himself, like an arrow shot at an ever decreasing bull's-eye, dived through the vanishing opening to land in the churned up slush waiting upon the other side.

"It's raining again," Corum said with a smile "and I never thought I would be as happy as I am now to feel it." Tablis also smiled and simply nodded.

They picked themselves up and looked behind them—Trackerman's caravan had disintegrated, wheels and axles shed and horses grazing in the distance. The clever box itself was now shrinking at a most incredible rate; soon it was no more than the size of a seaman's chest, and then a jewellery box.

"Time to vacate the vicinity I think, my Lord." They backed away.

"What will happen?" Corum asked as they retreated to the very edge of the field, where the woods began. The box was no longer visible.

"I'm not sure . . ." Tablis began, but he had no time to finish before there was an audible pop, and an implosion of air. They felt themselves momentarily being pulled towards the very centre of the field. This lasted barely a moment, however, before there was another crack of thunder and they were knocked onto their backs by the blast.

"It's gone," Tablis said, and there was almost a touch of disappointment in his voice.

"But where?"Corum asked.

Tablis just shook his head. "Perhaps the same place the Trackerman beast went."

"Do you really think so?"

Tablis nodded. "I hope so, my Lord" he said. "I really do."

* * *

Two riders in the rain, the small one spoke at last. "The men of Burgarach . . . ?" The question was left hanging.

"They will follow the magic fire-brand until it leads them back to their barracks, then it will fade; of their memory, I cannot be sure." Tablis shrugged; spray bounced off his shoulders.

Corum remembered something and dug into his pockets. "The stone," he said "I've still got the stone."

"Hang onto it, my Lord," Tablis smiled. "Think of it as a reminder of our adventures, a keepsake."

"But don't you wish it returned?"

Tablis shook his head. "No my Lord, I have a far greater reminder."

"The casting . . . ?" Corum asked.

Tablis smiled. "Yes, my Lord," he said. "It's a powerful magic—a Beast Stone. That such a thing should ever fall into my possession . . . ?" He just shook his head at the wonder of it all.

Corum also smiled to himself and placed the stone up against his left eye, closing his right.

"Just for old time's sake," he muttered, and wasn't surprised to see an unchanged view in front of him. He looked upwards, sweeping his gaze across a grey leaden sky; momentarily there was a flash of light and the great beast hiding behind the clouds was suddenly glimpsed, and then it was gone again. Corum shivered.

"See anything, my Lord?" Tablis asked him casually.

"No," Corum said stiffly, "not a thing." He returned the stone to his pocket, watching the ground before him, afraid now to return his gaze to the heavens. A nameless fear gripped him. It was then that he noticed for the first time since entering the Stealthlands the vaguest hint of a shadow, and Tablis's voice cheery in greeting.

"By the Abyss, my friend, at long last; I had forgotten you."

Corum looked up in surprise. The beast had returned.

Smiling, they rode on.

A Shadow Guard's Passing

I

In Kalishandra, the city of lost travellers, the city in the abyss, darkness has form. In the mist that rises periodically from cracks between the cobblestones, it has life. Melt-mist, the shaper, drifts along empty streets, welling into deep, choking pools in forgotten courtyards. It breaks in ephemeral smoke waves upon the stark stone walls of towers, which protrude above its curling tendrils like strangely envisaged nightmares. These bleak, inhospitable eyries are the lairs of dark and terrible wizards, beneath whose hard and stony gaze Kalishandra shifts. Streets change. Walls stand where before there was but open space. Courtyards once remembered fade into obscurity. Old things disappear, are misplaced; here a statue, there an ornamental fish pond. Even older thing return. The smell of a river long thought lost—blood upon the cobbles. It continues . . .

* * *

The eyes of Traxell the alchemist drift upon hidden currents, bobbing like brightly coloured corks throughout the length and breadth of the old Verinkad sector. Night eyes watch and wait should the mists bring forth something new; they see tower courtyards joined by defensive balustrades and narrow high-walled streets, walk walls and guard towers all mist shrouded. Nothing else, no movement. Nothing except . . .

"The fool is abroad," Traxell says to the shadow guard. "In the outer maze and during the height of the mists." He shakes his head in amazement. He is a small wizened figure with intelligent, green eyes and short jet hair. His purple robes were once all the fashion amongst the wealthy citizenry of Verinkad— and will be again when the mists rise. But until then, he must make do with the shadow guard. Its conversation is necessarily limited; but then, it is for listening that it is prized. They stand, motes in the golden background of the east window of his observatory tower, watching through his many night eyes as the fool makes his way through the melt-mist, rising slowly from the gloom of the lower levels.

In a narrow mist-ribboned laneway Engen fell, his great burnished breastplate striking the cobbles with a clang. There he lay, prone for a moment like an upturned tortoise, a shrunken figure within armour three sizes too large. His arms waggled disorientedly for a moment before he was able to lever himself upwards, like a statue slowly being pushed erect. His unhelmed profile, momentarily revealed, was that of a lost prince whose puzzled eyes forever scanned the mists.

Of all those travellers in Kalishandra, the wizard thinks to himself, half in scorn, half in sorrow, *Engen is the most lost of us all.* And as Traxell watches the knight-jester resume his bumbling progress through the mists, bumping into walls and falling over, he wonders once again as to his creator. Was it perhaps Maranon who first gave Engen life? Was he a plaything, something to make her laugh, to suit her sadistic games? Did she then cast him free in the city to find his own way—the ultimate joke! Then again, perhaps it had been Spandrell. But, no. His actions were far more predictable. Aggression without subtlety, that was his way. He had no time for such diversions. Nor was it likely to have been Hamada. And yet what did he really know of the Watcher, of any of them? They had all, at one time or another, been cast into this place, and come to know its darkness as home. In their own way they all had night eyes, even Engen.

Traxell steps away from the window and the shadow guard follows. The window immediately darkens as if a curtain had been dropped, giving the impression to any distant observers that a great golden eye had winked shut. The domed interior of Traxell's observatory is a jumble of strange equipment and magical vials filled with brightly-hued liquids. Suspended in the air above these, several dozen night eyes float serenely, their lids closed tight. The wizened alchemist scuttles about them like a purple bowerbird searching out its favourite baubles. All the while he keeps up a one-sided conversation with the shadow guard, which now floats by an alcove in the wall. In the very centre of the room, a spiral staircase leads downwards to the lower levels of Verinkad itself. A few wisps of mist can be seen reaching up this stairwell, only to writhe and die upon coming into contact with the antiseptic light from above.

"It appears worst in these the outer edges of the city,"Traxell says, half to himself and half to the shadow guard, "out here where the grey wastes are closest and getting closer all the time. I'm not sure if it's the city that's expanding outwards or if the grey areas themselves have advanced. Whichever is correct, we will soon be in a state of large-scale change. The melt-mists are already occurring with a greater regularity than ever before, and I fear for our long-term position in the city. My only consolation is that Spandrell is even closer to the edge than I. It will not go well for the necromancer this time, and that means more problems for us."

He points to the night eyes. "These must be positioned along the eastern boundary. Retreat three streets for safety and then follow the way mark as before. You have your orders!"

The shadow guard glides down the stairwell, the night eyes trailing behind like obedient pets. As they disappear from sight, Traxell sighs and returns to the window. Automatically it clears and he looks out. All is darkness, total and utter. He cannot see a thing. He knows that out there somewhere is a mass of vast sprawling cities, all segments of the one—Kalishandra! And out there are others like him; sorcerers, but with strange magic powers as, no doubt, his powers seem strange to them. A game of strength-testing is occurring. Although stalled now by the melt-mist, it will start up again soon enough; and for the losers, exile from the city would be the price of defeat. To be cast out again! He couldn't face that. *The grey wastes*! He blocks out the window and waits for the shadow guard's return.

*   *   *

Engen stumbled forward. The mist tormented him, walls that weren't, *walls that were, stone melted, stone gone. He fell against a wall; his face pressed against cold, hard stone. Real,* he thought. He grasped at it—real! He felt a sticky substance well against his cheek and along his arm. He looked up at the red globules dripping down on him from above—*blood*! Screaming masks stared down at him with sightless eyes atop their spikes. As he fell away from them back into the mists, he thought he heard them call out. The river called as well. He fell in.

II

THE MISTS HAD BEGUN TO clear, by the time the first signs of a new attack season began to reach him. Night eyes all along the outer defence walls had been blinded. He sent out the shadow guard to investigate; and through its specially adapted night eyes, it saw the Sternguard Towers that marked the boundaries of his defensive position. New eyes were quickly placed in readiness. Brief glimpses of sliver knives hade been the only warnings given; they had been far too quick for the sabotaged night eyes to counter. This was Spandrell's work, undoubtedly. Traxell had to find the necromancer's spell-bridge, and quickly, before he was able to send cargo through.

The shadow guard prowled. Up in his observatory tower Traxell fretted, pacing nervously.

Then action! A night eye was blinded beside a guard tower—and the projectile had apparently come from within.

Traxell/the shadow guard quickly arrived upon the scene, reinforcements in tow. And as he dispersed the tower, a raucous chanting could be heard.

"*A knife. Thrice.*"

Three weapons appeared in the space recently occupied by the tower; but before they could fall at the shadow guard, they were burnt in mid-air by the night eyes which turned a bright red. The chanting continued.

"*Small assassins, eye of flame, destroy this demon in thy name.*"

Small sword-carrying monsters came tumbling out as if from an upturned receptacle, but the night eyes burned them down even as they appeared. Traxell meanwhile tried to close the bridge from his end, calling on the same reserves of strength that Spandrell was expending to keep it open. Spandrell's reserves must have been fading though, because the chanting was becoming more distant, and the flood of vile weaponry through the gate had stemmed to a mere trickle. A final battalion of spinning knives appeared and was duly destroyed, all except for one which Traxell sent back through the now collapsing gate. A faint chuckle was heard at the other end, then the attack was over, and Spandrell's power drained.

After this, the real tower was returned and the night eyes dispersed. Although Traxell left several on guard at this position—just in case.

Spandrell rarely attacked the same place more than once; but it had been known to happen, and it was safer to take no risks. He sent the shadow guard to collect up the night eyes damaged in the attack, and counted his losses.

In the outer edges of Verinkad, melt-season had washed some of his more marginal defences away. Strange new structures now took their place. The city had shifted again—only marginally perhaps, but still, enough; and once more he had been a loser.

III

THERE WAS ALWAYS SOMETHING NEW in the city. But this time it was different; he sensed it. Like the somnolent thoughts of some sleeping giant, they reverberated around Kalishandra; neither words, exactly, nor visions, but vague feelings of dread and fear. They became increasingly and inevitably more unsettling, like the slow tolling of a warning bell echoing out across the city.

Traxell, high up in his observatory, felt them and shivered— as no doubt did Spandrell, plotting in his madman's bunker. And the others also heard the city's call; Hamada in his watcher's castle, resplendent in his cosmetic blindness, the jewelled hilt of the dagger protruding just above his breastbone . . . Maranon in her mauve sector, with its purple mist and the green-eyed sharp-clawed familiars, forever prowling the ghostly alleyways. It was heard by the masters of those other places where his prying night eyes had as yet failed to reach, those beyond Kira Ull Ziat, the first city, around which they all clung like uncertain children. It was heard even by the unknown master of them all; whose dark towers dwarfed even the mightiest of their constructions, and from whose unaltering laws there appeared no escape. Not even their combined efforts in the past had been able to bring about the arrival of a false dawn to Kalishandra. And now had come this! He knew the fear he was experiencing was merely a prelude, for a part of the city was to die. In its own inscrutable way, Kalishandra had spoken.

Traxell, watching Engen make his customary bumbling raid through the outer courtyards and towards the very centre of old Verinkad itself, felt curiously pleased; almost as if the fool's reappearance was a signal that in his corner of Kalishandra, at least, all was well. Perhaps it was this feeling of relief that made him still his hand. Rarely if ever had he allowed the fool to penetrate this far into his territories. Usually he had the night eyes kill him as soon as he reached the first way mark; but like an often exorcised ghost, he always returned. Somewhere out there in the darkness, in the ever changing marginals, someone believed in him sufficiently to cause reanimation time and again. He was Kalishandra's court jester, a plaything of wizards— Engen would have to be eliminated. This time, however, he chose to use the shadow guard.

Upon sighting the shadow guard, Engen immediately drew his sword. His obvious intent was to slay the demon where it stood. However his dreams of glory were to be short-lived as he found his sword blade suddenly turned to putty. Showing great presence of mind, he tried to hit the shadow guard with its hilt. The force of the blow was so great that the newly reformed steel sliced off the unfortunate knight's hand, and it fell to the ground where it lay flopping like a stranded fish.

Traxell recalled the shadow guard in disgust, thinking to himself; why waste its time on such a mission? Engen was a danger only to himself; and anyway, showing such perseverance, he had deserved to get this far. Traxell decided he would leave a night eye to track him further, and he wouldn't kill him—not just yet.

Engen's attempts at staunching the flow of blood by rejoining the hand finally succeeded. But unfortunately for him, with all the excitement his sense of direction seemed to have become confused, for he left the courtyard by the way he had entered it—as always, undaunted.

IV

HAVEN—TRAXELL'S VERINKAD REVIVED. A PLACE of great merchant palaces—streets where careful handlers, crusty captains and impatient silks live momentarily, like some preconceived vision of truth, in a land where truth can but shift and change. He immerses himself in it. A thousand ghosts of people who never were appear on his streets. His is a stylised view of the past, of a Verinkad seen only in his dreams. The reality is now only a distant memory, and can never be recalled. So he must make do with what is left—the dreams. He loses himself in them. As the shadow guard, he walks the streets of his city as a god might walk amongst those of his creations. For a moment he may forget his worries and hide in the safety of his personal fantasy. But for how long? The night eyes remain as a salient reminder of the darker things, their strangely threatening presence only enhanced by the otherwise normality of the scenes now surrounding him. The ghosts upon the streets may not see the truths that remain hidden, but he can.

A voice! Was that a voice?

The night eyes remain clear.

"Break, kill, fire, burn."

No, nothing. There's nothing out there. Voices from the crowd. That's all. Voices of the dead echoing back at him, reassuring, confident, supportive—but dead.

No change. The eyes remain clear.

Upon a distant cobbled street, shadows coalesce, as if drawn together from the very night. It moves towards the first balustrade and passes through.

Still the eyes remain clear!

Blue silks walk the streets. The handlers grunt with their sweaty exertions and laugh. In the taverns crude songs are sung. Through it all the shadow guard passes without a sound. Parts of the city have already begun to decay, and many of the people not already vanished are starting to step out of their predestined rolls. A new city is forming within the old; characteristics are beginning to change. Here and there the very essence of Verinkad has begun to be inadvertently shaped by those moving within it. A type of awakening of self-consciousness is occurring. Though still in its infancy, and doomed by the melt-mists to premature extinction, it is nevertheless a remarkable happening. To the shadow guard, unaware of anything except on the most basic level, it means that as it careers through Verinkad, uncontrolled and uncontrollable, bouncing off walls and towers, sometimes and increasingly so, it is able to pass itself through.

Sail On, Sail On

I

ARRON CEDRIS HAD ALWAYS HAD talented hands. When he was a mere child his mother often speculated that he would grow up to be a great painter, or perhaps a sculptor, a shaper of stone. His father, a more practical soul, had pointed him in the direction of stonemasonry. Cedris had become, in his own terms, a great artist, a shaper of flesh. In his finely balanced hand a rapier blade could pluck the eyeball from the socket of an adversary with nary a brush against cheek or nose, slice open a man's lip for insult real or imagined, or find the chink in the tightest woven chain mail. It was said of him that he could kill a man with such surreptitious skill that the victim himself would remain unaware. It was also said that he liked to kill. Moreover it was inferred, never spoken outwardly, for to do so invited a swift and certain doom, that his blade provided him with his only form of release. He was a man to be deferred to, feared, respected in his fashion, but never admired, looked up to or loved. To some he might have cut a sad figure, had they observed him closely this day. Yet close observation was for the brave, the naïve or the foolhardy, and there were few of those in Zes Farrin upon a summer's morn when other tasks beckoned. Few to stand idly by and watch the carefully stated saunter of a hired killer prowling restlessly a city whose backstreets he knew as well as any of the rats that scuttled out of the sewers and canals, stinking of excreta.

As Cedris passed along the narrow cobble-stone lanes, between the crowded sandstone buildings that rose three and four storeys above him, women in bright dresses and scarves standing upon ancient wrought iron balconies conversed with neighbours while nursing babies or setting washing. They ignored him, continuing their talk, only their eyes betrayed them, turning imperceptibly downwards, their faces allowing briefly expressions of disgust. A man walking in the opposite direction stepped aside with practised ease. Cedris fingered his scabbard and stopped briefly, his prominent nose in the air, letting the heady vapours from the surrounding scent lanterns bring forth their own memories.

Jervic! He had finished him here, against that far wall, his rapier through his throat, pinning him like an insect in a collector's case. It had been fully two years before, but whenever he smelt that sweet concoction, rose petals, lavender flowers and mint, it all returned. He smiled to himself in secret triumph, patted his scabbard like a faithful dog, and began to walk onwards.

His attention momentarily held by his reverie, he failed to take notice of the shadow in a half open doorway, which observed this ritual reliving with interest. The shadow noted Cedris's jaunty manner and journeyman's clothes. Cedris was clean shaven and his hair was damp and slicked back, as if he had simply placed his head within a washing bowl and then combed it into place. He was all blacks and browns. Should he turn suddenly, the strips of material about his belt would rise like a series of ribbons and flutter about. Each flap of material was written upon in a spidery hand, though what they signified the shadow couldn't make out; but it could guess. Cedris was like a child reliving and revelling in his victories; it could imagine him leading an unwilling spectator upon a gruesome historical tour of the city.

Here he had disposed of so and so, disembowelling him, and here another, piercing his brain through the left nostril, and again, this time penetrating the heart via a gap in the chain mail under the arm. If the shadow could have smiled to itself it would have, but instead it flowed out of the doorway, taking briefly the shadow-form of a dark winged hawk, and set off after Cedris.

The instincts of a sword carrier are highly sensitized, and Cedris more than most tasted danger in the air as might a snake. He turned around, hand upon the hilt of his sword. The alleyway behind him remained empty. He blinked! A shadow raced towards him across the cobbles, a large black bird. Instinctively he glanced upwards—the strip of sky between the sandstone bluffs remained a clear blue. He looked down in time to see the shadow almost upon him, and was just about to glance up again in another attempt to find the bird, when something struck him very hard in the stomach. It knocked him onto his back and when he sat up he saw a black knife embedded in his gut. Even as he watched spellbound, yet horrified, it twisted itself in deeper, until soon only the tail end of the handle showed. There was neither blood nor great pain, only a spreading numbness. He tried to reach out with his hands and pull it free, but they refused to move—he was cast as in stone. Darkness collapsed in on him.

* * *

To those watching from their balconies above, the scene must have been one of comical delight. The feared and loathed Arron Cedris set upon his rump by a passing bird. A hawk, some said later, discussing the strange happening, or a crow. Still others claimed that it hadn't been a bird at all, but a large black dog. One thing they could all agree on, however, was the puzzling finale to the episode. After Cedris had gotten almost sheepishly to his feet and slunk off, there had remained a dark mark upon the cobbles, like a blood stain. It had faded after a few minutes, so its true nature was uncertain.

II

MORNING BROUGHT THE SMELL OF the canals, a putrid stink of defecation and decay; it also brought the water carrier.

Brandel Trengarth, sitting before the misted window, saw the small figure making his way up the cobbled laneway, hobbling slightly, the twin buckets balanced by a stick resting upon his skinny shoulders. Trengarth tried rubbing the glass clear to gain a better view, but the scene remained misted, as if the figure itself was merely a product of the early morning air, and would burn away like so much wispy cloud with the arrival of the sun. Trengarth knew better, however, for this was no simple apparition.

The water carrier stopped in front of Trengarth's rooms and peered upwards. In response, Trengarth opened the window and poked his head out into the cold, crisp morning air. His view of the water carrier's face was now much improved. He could see the features of a young boy, sandy hair, skinny strong limbs dressed in rags. His left foot sported a battered leather shoe, while the right, a club foot, was swathed in tight strips of sackcloth. The water carrier didn't appear to see him; he never did.

Trengarth now felt the ghostly presence of the other—the Bonegrinder, pass across him as if an eclipse. He saw his own fingers gripping the windowsill, covered by a wrinkled parchment skin, old gnarled hands, gripping at first, then moving like a blur of wings against his eyes—beckoning.

He felt dizzy. Something moved in front of his face, and he had to turn away, stumble from the window through the chaos of his studio, past scattered paintings, discarded sketches and rolled canvases. He bumped into an easel and sent it crashing. No escape, he knew.

He entered another room; this one contained a papier-mâché reproduction of the city of Zes Farrin, in miniature. For a moment he towered above it, dwarfing walls and fortifications, a malign shadow reaching out to engulf its unseen inhabitants. But he tallied here not, for the smell of the canals grew ever stronger, and he knew what that signified.

He found the mirror at last and steadied himself before its reassuring reflection.

Brandel Trengarth lives; he thought decisively; he was no ghost. The mirror showed a tall man in a paint-spattered white nightshirt that hung down to his ankles. His face was drawn and haggard. Brown curly hair ran amok past his shoulders and its fringe was brushed with paint flecks, where he had come too close to a newly completed canvas. He often bumped into things now. The dreaming winds had left him unable to escape these visions; they ruled him, entrapped him within cities he knew, yet didn't; Zes Farrin, its streets, markets and walls, but worst of all his own rooms. No, he realized, not his, the one who in this other city lived in these rooms, the one he knew only as the Bonegrinder—the magic man.

The mirror was clouding over now; it was starting in earnest and there was nothing he could do. The stench of defecation overwhelmed him.

*   *   *

Hallis waited for the Bonegrinder's signal, then leaving one of his buckets without, he entered the old shaman's house.

The lower storey was emptied of furniture, but filled with other much stranger objects. The towers of salt guarding the various doorways had crumbled somewhat, since his last visit, and the intricate strings of many coloured pouches, filled with various herbs, had come adrift of their fastenings like wayward streamers and crashed to the floor, some of them breaking open upon impact and scattering their contents upon the cracking tiles. Moisture seemed to be seeping up through the floor and into the very walls. The vile smell of the canals was stronger now than ever before. Hallis observed these developments with dismay.

He carried his remaining bucket to the staircase, hoping that in the intervening time it too hadn't been sabotaged by the vapours the Bonegrinder's enemies sent against him, spirits of dankness and decay, rotting and putrefying all they touched.

But the staircase, he noted, despite its outward appearance, was of sturdy construction and would hold up for some time yet.

As he began to climb, the entire house seemed to creak; pieces of damp plaster from the ceiling dropped upon him, leaving smears of black in their place. He reached the second storey, and spied the collection of copper artefacts spread out across the floor. The slow spread of the verdigris from the furthest part of the house, that nearest the canal, toward the far wing where the Bonegrinder had retreated, charted the spread of the malign influence.

"They have called forth a spirit of the blackness, a foul thing from the depths of the canals." The Bonegrinder's voice raged as by way of greeting. "They send it against me again and again. What say you, Hallis, do I stand or fall?"

"You stand, master," Hallis said, following the voice into the room from which it emanated. "But your defences below are raddled."

The far wing of the Bonegrinder's house overlooked the street by way of a single window. The room itself was a battleground. The walls were kinked, the plaster coming away in circular clumps, exposing the stone beyond, like skin peeled back to reveal the bone. *There are blotches upon the skin of this house*, Hallis thought, strange circular water marks, as if the malformed footprints of monsters approaching the Bonegrinder steadily across the ceiling and walls. The floor, however, was covered in layers of crushed herbs and double lines of salt towers. In the corner in which Hallis stood, the herbs were rotted and blackened, the salt towers melted and crumbling, the smell of faeces overpowering. Further towards the middle of the room the protective measures were still intact, and beyond this the Bonegrinder sheltered.

"You had no problems reaching the house?" he asked.

Hallis shook his head and lowered his bucket. "The streets are quiet; I saw no sign of the Goldenreds or their handiwork."

"The fetch was about last night," the Bonegrinder informed him. "I heard it out in the street; I believe I drove it off with the Eye, but it must be out there somewhere. I fear it will come looking for you, Hallis, now that they know you are assisting me."

The water carrier swallowed nervously. The short squat figure of the Bonegrinder sat in a beam of light from the open window, his bald head glistening. He was naked except for his loin cloth, his body skeletal thin and covered in scars, many of them seemingly of a recent vintage, and deep. His green eyes, however, were friendly and alive.

"You should be keen to be away, my young friend, before it returns."

Hallis nodded. "But I will be back in three days time, as usual." He made his voice sound more determined than he felt.

The Bonegrinder didn't laugh at his false bravado, but shook his head seriously. "You are strong-willed, Hallis, but alas foolish also. You can see the way the battle goes."

"You stand!" Hallis interrupted. "Still you stand."

"Yes, still I stand," the Bonegrinder roared, "but for how long, eh? Look all about you. Well, boy, what do you see?" His voice softened. "I tire, you see, Hallis. Each time it comes for me it has advanced further into the house. No combination of incense and spell can keep it at bay forever, and when it reaches me, Hallis, I shall die as certainly as if they had come and struck me down themselves."

"Then you must come with me," Hallis implored him. "I will help you; once you leave this house you will be able to fight them."

"No!" The Bonegrinder lifted a withered hand. "I shall do my fighting here. The city remains under siege, so I am trapped. This house is mine, even now; it holds a magic, Hallis, and there are still options open to me." He smiled and pointed to a series of Illwisher's cards upon the floor in a circle around him. Each one was imprinted with a bloodied thumbprint and a teaspoon heaping of a peppery substance.

"I shall cleanse this house before I go, cleanse it for all time."

"And what of me . . . ?" Hallis asked sadly.

"You mustn't return here; it will be too dangerous. Leave the bucket and go now; you have done all that you can, more so, in fact. As for the siege I can promise nothing; there are great forces at work. I have done what I can, but there are bad times ahead for all of us."

Hallis was about to turn and leave when the Bonegrinder seemed to remember something, and reached into one of a collection of pouches upon the floor beside him. He removed the skull of a small animal and tossed it to Hallis, who caught it with a puzzled frown.

"What's this?" he asked.

"A gift," the Bonegrinder said. "I shan't need him anymore."

"Him . . . ?"

"Watch out for the fetch, Hallis," he only said, smiling. "Hurry now, enemies both without and within are stirring."

*   *   *

Brandel Trengarth stood at his window and watched the small figure of the water carrier leave. How long he had been standing here he had no idea. Hallis was starting to fade now, as he limped away up the street, his outline blurring, becoming a mirage, leaving a shimmering silvery light, that caused Trengarth's eyes to water and forced him to rub them with his fists. When he opened them again the street was quiet and empty. The Zes Farrin that Trengarth knew and loved had returned, but for how long?

III

TRENGARTH DECIDED TO ESCAPE THE malign influence of the house for a time; its feeling of entrapment was ever present. It had reached a point where he confined himself more and more often, these days, to that one small section of the house that the Bonegrinder himself had retreated into, sitting at the window and staring out upon his city, as if he too were under some form of siege.

Yet when he entered the wider city the madness didn't end; it just changed in nature. In the markets, for example, as he wended his way between the closely packed stalls, he noted the usual quota of raised eyebrows and whispered asides. *Even a madman must eat*, he thought without bitterness, *or do they fear to catch my insanity as one would a skin disease?* They still accepted his coin, however; there was no biting or weighing, so perhaps a little of his good name remained.

This time only one man indulged in what in previous times had been thought quite a game, the questioning, usually in a voice dripping sarcasm, of the madman Trengarth upon the state of the siege. Trengarth remained calm, as he had always done, and simply informed him of what he knew, that the enemies' camp had been reinforced and that there were fresh raids upon the southern wall.

In black tunic and matching breeches, with white ruffles at the shirt sleeve and polished silver buttons, Trengarth remained to the populace of Zes Farrin a dandy in aspect, if no longer in fact. The man reddened somewhat, and scurried away, as if surprised at the sheer insufferable conviction in Trengarth's words. Well used to such responses, he smiled inwardly and left the markets, to the jeering of a group of children who traditionally followed him all the way to Tockhaven square, calling out rude names and inviting him to show them where the enemy hid, so they could slay them. They often carried wooden swords and home-made shields; the resultant procession looking like some bizarre crusade. Yet this time they followed him for only a short distance before, in response to some secret signal, they pelted him with small stones, then melted away, sensing perhaps a sea change. *Odd,* he thought, slightly puzzled, for it was not yet the ebb tide's run; the residents of Zes Farrin were well used to organizing their lives around the discharges that accompanied their tidal canal's ebb.

Zes Farrin, Trengarth thought in civic self-satisfaction, was a city of scents and perfumes. Here all manner of scents could be appreciated as one walked through the back alleys of the city. The scent lanterns were an integral part of the city's identity, so much so, in fact, that one with sufficient knowledge could walk blindfolded, led by the hand of a stranger, and inform him by smell alone where within the city they now stood. Each section of Zes Farrin had its own traditions in the way of incense and perfume, and stuck to them rigidly. So, when the evil smelling vapours from the canals did arrive, with their tainting breath and fouling touch, washing would be gone, windows closed, doors shut and scent lanterns withdrawn with their owners to the safety of their houses. Only those with strong stomachs, debased nasal capacities, and poorly paid menial jobs would be out in it—the three things tended to go together in Zes Farrin. Elaborately carved boxes of snuff and smelling salts were as common to these men as the pox, and were produced frequently.

As it was, Trengarth, lost in contemplation, reached the Mazuarine quarter before he realized he was again being followed. The stink of the canals was suddenly about him, as if he had stepped into a pocket of dead air. The very atmosphere seemed to thicken with moisture and decay. The sunlight, beating down upon him only moments before, now seemed somehow diffuse, a pallid impostor.

He hurried forward with renewed purpose, hoping to quickly reach the other side of this unwelcome black spot, and noticed with some surprise as he glanced back, that the man trailing him continued to do so despite his entering such an area. The figure began to blur, however, as if he were observing it through an out of focus lens.

He hurried down a flight of steps, noticing that there was a sunken courtyard to his right that he couldn't remember ever seeing before. Here figures moved about a vast banqueting table; the sun was emerging again and reflected upon their feast. Nine men in robes all the colours of the rainbow repositioned themselves in poses of excess, then, as if waking from a reverie, they chanted in unison before again varying their pose—a tilt of the hand or head, a golden goblet lifted higher. The chanting began again.

Trengarth reached the base of the steps and found his view blocked by a stone wall. He turned about as there came from behind him a clattering sound. He thought of the sinister figure trailing him, and momentarily his heart leapt.

Something small and dark tumbled down the final step and came to rest at his feet, covered in a coating of black slime. Despite its appearance, its origins were quite apparent; it was a ball of string wound about either a piece of bone or a small bottle. He noticed now the slimy trail made by the fraying, as it had somehow managed to unravel while rolling down the stairs. He followed the trail back to its source, re-climbing like a man taking his final steps to the gallows. The stone wall that he had originally thought started near the base of the stairs, shadowed the stairway nearly all the way down, being the hidden side of a group of extremely real houses. The sunken courtyard had merely been a hallucination; or had it?

He bent down to where the beginnings of the string emerged from an otherwise featureless wall; it broke apart at his touch, and he smeared it across the stone until it left a grey-green stain. He thought of the way it might have been thrown, spinning in the air as it unravelled, passing through stone that wasn't always stone—a sea change—many cities, many times. He ran his hand along the cold surface of the wall, sensing its sturdy and considerable presence, its history. The ball of string was equally and undeniably part of the present.

Cupping it safely in his grasp, he tried to find his way home, but it no longer seemed as easy as before. He took several wrong turns and it was only the familiar scents of the Galiese sector that finally guided him back. In this period of disconnected wandering, he had seen other things which disturbed him. For a time he thought that the dreaming winds had returned—he saw himself in a torn salmon shirt and kilt, fringed with golden tassels. His feet had been bare and bloodied, as if he had trodden on thorns or broken glass. A line of people had filed past him, one at a time, kneeling to pluck a tassel from his kilt and then bending down to kiss the anointed stones. There had been mist everywhere and he had been moving through it, but others too were lost; he had caught another glimpse of the man who had been following him earlier. A short rapier drawn, he was creeping along pressed close up to the walls, like a sleek brown cat, his hair slicked back and his eyes locked forever upon something just out of sight. There was a furtiveness about him that instilled doubt over his situation; was it the hunter he played, or the hunted?

Trengarth at last found sanctuary within his room, locking his door upon the madness without, only to be confronted by that which had been awaiting his return. Once again the smell of the canals assailed him.

IV

A SHADOW TOWERED ABOVE ZES Farrin, dwarfing its walls, towers, fortifications, a gigantic hand reaching out towards the city, fingers spread. The shadow of its thumb intersected in the quarter of Galiese with a house unremarkable from all its fellows.

Flames burst forth as if from some hidden reservoir, until the Bonegrinder was surrounded by a wall of fire. Foul shadows impaled upon the flames writhed, turning to ash and falling upon the Bonegrinder's newly re-opened stigmata. A man tarred in blood and feathered in the ash of his enemies, he sat unmoved while the illwisher's cards continued to issue forth flame, though they blackened not. The floor and ceiling now began to catch alight.

The hand wavered for a moment, and the flames decreased, allowing an observer, had there been one, a brief glimpse of the cards.

THE BROKEN TOWER—two towers, one in the shadowfall of the other; where the shadow touched the second tower decay had set in, windows broken, stone crumbling.

THE KING IN RED AND BLACK—here a regal figure with a crown of golden thorns lay upon a bier of animal skins, their heads still attached, hanging down like oversized medallions. The audience themselves wore masks and stood with their backs to the bier, staring out at the observer—flame issued from their mouths.

The ceiling caved in.

The hand moved on, its shadowfall passing like a dark wing out across Zes Farrin. As night fell the thumb settled upon Ankhosa, city of the dead, city within a city. Here grave houses were shrouded in night fog and silence; in some up to eight generations lay entombed. The hand found the one it wanted— movement within, hidden ceremonies, candles flickering in the darkness, a soft chanting. There were eight men in golden uniforms and blood red habits, a ninth lying upon a resting stone. Draped in a tapestry depicting the feast of the nine, this man cast no shadow and his eyes were empty, yet he was not dead. The chanting continued.

A small figure had crawled to the top of the gently gabled roof of the grave house, and removed a piece of tiling to watch the proceedings below. Hallis, his eyes bright and frightened, yet there was a determined set to his jaw and he held the small bone skull tied up with string. His thoughts were illuminating; they contained visions of a ship of green fire. He didn't know why he saw the ship, but he saw it often now; sometimes he was the only one on board, other times the Bonegrinder too was there and sometimes others he didn't know. Most often there was a tall man with dark curly hair who stood at the prow like a masthead, staring out into the grey mists through which the ship moved. He thought of the ship now; he believed it would carry him when he died; he wanted to believe this, especially now.

He took a deep breath and begins to lower the bone skull down towards where the Goldenred lay upon the tapestry. It got halfway down before one of the surrounding eight noticed its oddly shaped shadow, convergent upon the chest of their companion. Hallis let it drop all the way; the thread rapidly vanished, until the bone skull struck the chest of the Goldenred with a hollow thud.

Something screamed. Rings of smoke emerged as the body thrashed about in an uncoordinated attempt to throw off the fetish, which in the eerie candlelight of the tomb seemed to have come alive, a thin wiry stoat-like creature, tearing at the man's throat. The others converged, grasping at it, but Hallis was already pulling it away, drawing it back up towards him. The body below was torn and bleeding, but its shadow was returning—the fetch recalled. He had forced them to break off whatever task they had it performing. Hallis, despite the imminent danger, felt a thrill of achievement; he had trumped them. Now he had only to get away, before it recovered enough to be sent after him. Hopefully he had wounded it mortally, but he couldn't take the chance.

Stuffing the bloodied skull, string and all into a pouch he wore around his neck, he scrambled along the roof of the grave house to where it connected with the next one. A group of five or six interconnected grave houses could be covered in quick time, by a person as used to clambering about them as Hallis was. With his club foot, Hallis found roof travel far preferable to the fast shuffle that was the best he could manage at ground level. His hands were strong and dexterous, like a climbing monkey's, and he quickly put two dozen grave houses between himself and the Goldenreds. He had to jump across several miniature laneways and change streets, but he heard no sound of pursuit, which perversely worried him. It was far preferable to have the Goldenreds scouring the streets below in a fruitless search, than repairing their fetch. Hallis slowed his flight to a steady pace, clambering between decaying statues and decorative minarets. Occasionally he disturbed nesting birds or roosting bats, and each time he would stop to see if the noise had initiated signs of pursuit. But no, the city of the dead remained just that. If anything moved in its miniature replica streets and bazaars then it was only the ghosts Ankhosa had been originally constructed for.

V

TRENGARTH AWOKE TO FIND HIMSELF sprawled like a broken giant before the walls of his papier-mâché Zes Farrin, one bloodied hand grasping for the remains of the bone skull scattered across the floor about him. Daubs of blood lodged upon the walls, glistening; others had landed within the city itself. Pieces of broken, slime-covered bone adhered bloodily to the great gates, whilst the south tower showed every sign of suffering whiplash. Had the skull exploded, or simply shattered violently upon his fall? Either way it had made a mess of his hand; the bleeding appeared difficult to stem. Was it possible an artery had been severed?

He scrambled to his feet, the replica Zes Farrin blurring beneath his unsteady gaze, its streets and buildings shifting unsettlingly. He turned away, all the madness momentarily forgotten, in his concern for his wound. He would need to bind it with something; cloth would be preferable.

He hurried into his studio, where he knew his discarded nightshirt lay in a crumpled white heap. It was by the window, and as he reached out for it he saw the figure in the street below, the same one he had first seen following him in the Mazuarine. He was pacing back and forth beneath Trengarth's window, fingering the hilt of his sword, as if continuing to assure himself of its presence.

Trengarth gripped the windowsill in anxious anticipation, cursing that day he had been caught in the dreaming winds, those once in a generation southerlies that blew in from the empty areas of the map, the dead places, bringing visions and memories of things thought long buried. The names of strange, impossible cities lingered in his mind, like whispered spell casts, Kalishandra, Toll Armon, Verinkad. They were like objects for so long buried beneath a shifting desert sand, no sooner uncovered than lost again, so that only a hint of their grandeur lingered, a tantalizing evocative scent.

A general madness had swept the city for the duration, but few had shown signs of long-term effects, Trengarth excepted; for him the dreaming had just begun. And now it appeared that the long siege was about to end, one way or another.

He was not surprised to see that his wounds had stopped bleeding. He thought of the Bonegrinder and dropped the night shirt; it was now soiled with blood and grime. The white cloth was like mist slowly clearing; within it he could see the banqueting table and the nine; eight were stilled now and the last one varying his pose in minute detail. In the background, shadows were just beginning to take shape; then he could see no more. The nightshirt was only a soiled cloth, and outside in the street the sword carrier continued to pace. Still, the message had been clear; he had to stop the feast of the nine, somehow.

*   *   *

Confronted at last with a chance to act, Trengarth did not hesitate. The city was imperilled in some way; although he didn't really understand, the feast and the treachery of the Goldenreds had something to do with it. The siege without would be assisted from within; the Goldenreds would throw open the gates to allow the enemy access to Zes Farrin. The enemy! He thought of massed men at arms, battle horses and camp fires at night for as far as the eye could see. Yet, another part of him saw only drifting mist. He was standing upon high, and the mist was swirling about him; he was looking for something, but the mist blanketed everything.

He shook his head, banishing such indecisive imagery. He had his calling, so now he moved quickly to prepare himself for the ordeal ahead.

Moving a large porcelain bath filled with rolled up canvases, he opened a cupboard long disused and peered within. Hidden amongst provincial travellers' garments and heavy ugly cloaks, a sword leaned. Its scabbard was tackily imbued with glass imitation precious stones, their surfaces cracked like crazy paving, and several empty holes where some had fallen out. He took it in his hand, surprised now by the memory of its weight. He drew its blade. It was flat and unimpressive; like a sick man's tongue it had developed a sort of grey-green patina. He wiped it clear with his nightshirt, thinking wryly that it was the first time this blade had tasted blood, and how typical that it should be his own. Yet even in this he found comfort, a sort of reverse symbolism. Whichever way he looked at it he was the chosen, the city's champion.

Tossing the scabbard back into the cupboard with some embarrassment, he tried some clumsy passes with the blade, affecting a dancer's stance, upon the tips of his toes. Unfortunately the blade remained too heavy for him, and he tended to topple forward at the end of each thrust. He shrugged his shoulders and decided to apply a flat-footed approach; he would trust to providence, and the support of the city.

He started downstairs, cradling the sword like a child, and observing the ancient scar tissue crisscrossing his hand like a cryptic message. His ruffled cuffs were now stiff with dried blood, and reminded him of intertwined red and white roses.

He unbolted the door and stepped out into the street; no courtiers, no trumpets, just an unremarkable laneway and the oddly-apparelled sword carrier.

Trengarth hefted his blade and stepped purposely forward, adopting a two-handed grip. With almost imperceptible effort the sword carrier lunged at him, the loose strips of material at his waist fluttering. Trengarth tried to parry, but the man was a blur of movement. In a moment he had retreated again, sword bloodied. Trengarth refused to look down, keeping his attention instead upon the point of his own sword. He held it out before him, as if offering its service as a hat rack.

The sword carrier observed him with a lack of emotion that was worse even than distain. Trengarth began to step towards him, tentatively, uncertainly, as if every step was a physical revelation.

Still he did not dare look down, but the hands holding the sword began to shake. Soon he was going to fall over, he knew, and when that happened he wouldn't be able to get back up. The sword carrier circled to the right, watching him all the while. Trengarth tried to turn with him, but strangely found this movement almost impossible.

His eyesight was going on him now; a grey mist was rising up as if from between the very cobbles themselves. His adversary was gone, stepping out of his view as if from within a picture frame.

He lost a grip upon his sword. He heard it clang dully upon the cobble-stones beneath him, as he sank to his knees.

I tried my best, he thought at last, as if in valediction. They could have asked no more, the Bonegrinder, Hallis. He was only sorry he couldn't stop the feast.

The mist rose up again and consumed him.

*　　*　　*

Trengarth is once again in the city, the Zes Farrin that isn't Zes Farrin. He runs, and the water carrier is there beside him—his club foot now healed.

They run together, their footfalls echoing in the empty silence—swords in their hands. They rush to the defence of the walls, through ever changing streets, the ghosts of the living and the dead.

For how else can you justify this tragedy?

A king in rags and chains . . .

A sword broken.

Mist rise in Kalishandra.

End Game

I

"THE FACT OF THE DYING changed nothing." Pallas spoke the words as would a judge delivering his verdict and Hallows, as the defendant, knew the punishment could only be death. "Do you want me to continue?" Pallas seemed uncertain. He held the piece of paper nervously, as if he feared the words it contained.

"Go ahead," Hallows assured him, ashen faced. "I need to hear it all."

"Are you sure?"

Hallows nodded. Clenching and unclenching his fists he wished he were holding a knife, so that he could cut himself, a symbolic offering to the altar of his failure.

Pallas spoke slowly, reading the words as if they were reluctantly given. A big man, as blond as Hallows was dark, his presence as guardian, food provider and companion through three different safe houses up to this point had been invaluable to Hallows' state of mind, yet was he also to be executioner?

"The judgement reads," Pallas said, "the killing of the poet Raab upon Merrywent Parade by our once brother Hallows was neither sanctioned by the Lords of Chaos nor assisted therein. Hallows' claim to have killed the third king is both delusional upon his part and proven falsehood—the fact of the dying changed nothing. The actions of this renegade, whose links with this guild, however tenuous, and although severed long ago, can no longer be ignored. To this end we announce the placing of a bounty upon the head of Hallows—a common murderer who hides his crime behind the mask of chivalry. He is not the knight who has slain the fabulous beast-king, but a madman intent upon undermining our guild. Brothers and sisters, look to your windows!"

"That's it," Hallows exclaimed. "The sound of knives being unsheathed."

Pallas shrugged. "They are just covering themselves."

"*They?*" Hallows laughed bitterly. "Surely you mean *we?*"

But Pallas just shook his head. "I don't know what to say. If it were up to me . . ."

"But it isn't," Hallows snapped, then caught himself. "I'm sorry, my friend, it's just the way they've done it—casting me adrift as if I were some sort of leper. The death was sanctioned; you know that."

Pallas nodded.

"I was encouraged to see beyond the man to spot the power within. Pallas—I swear to you—that poet was one of them. There were so many clues, the way his associates moved about him as if he were the fulcrum, the silent controller . . . Have you read Tamarin?"

Pallas smiled sadly, allowing Hallows' nervous energy to wash over him. "Yes, *Hunting the Shadow.* I can never forget it."

"Then you'll know the importance of the king and his surroundings, how one always influences the other, no matter how careful the king. Remember how the second king had taken the form of a rat catcher in Sudima?" Hallows was walking about the small room now, avoiding chairs and table while waving his hands in excitement, a smile of simple pleasure upon his face. "Tamarin had tracked him to the slush and rubbish-filled back streets of the poor quarter; remember that?"

Pallas was also smiling now. "Yes, the confrontation with the king's dogs, the way they grew in size and spat fire at him—gargoyle-like monsters."

"He only got away by entering the sewers," Hallows continued. "The pursuing animals could not ignore their instincts and became sidetracked by the presence of so many rats. That was what I liked most about Tamarin," Hallows said. "The way he could think his way out of a crisis. What do you think he'd make of this, eh?" Hallows found himself at the window now, looking out upon a narrow back alley.

"I'm not sure." Pallas' voice was sombre once more. "In *Hunting the Shadow* he did admit to three innocent killings, but he didn't go into exact details."

"Of course not," Hallows snapped. "But I know what he would have said—freedom from tyranny can only be bought with blood. But whose blood, eh? That is the question, Pallas."

Hallows turned to confront him. "Tell me the truth, my friend. Are you my executioner?"

Pallas paled, and this was answer enough.

"But there will be an executioner?"

This time Pallas nodded. "The posters and flyers have appeared already. They were mostly torn down by the pikemen before the arrival of the dawn, but this morning the streets were full of whispered half-conversations and unspoken signals. I saw many small squares of paper changing hands."

"Could they have been the lists of names?" Hallows questioned.

"I'm afraid not," Pallas admitted. "There was only one name upon their lips."

"So it has come to this—The hunt!"

Pallas couldn't hold his gaze. He looked forlornly at the floor.

"Tell me, Pallas, one last thing: how long do you think I have?"

"Not long," Pallas said, a trace of nervousness entering his voice. "The guild will send their man. If you wish to survive until nightfall I suggest you leave this place, and quickly. I can say no more. What I have told you already may cost my life." With this he collected his cloak and was heading for the door, when Hallows called out to him.

"Here, Pallas." He tossed him a small sabretache he had unclipped from his belt.

"What's in here?" Pallas asked as he lifted the flap.

"*Hunting the Shadow*!" Hallows smiled. "Tamarin's manifesto."

"But you'll . . ."

"What use is it to me now? Go now before the executioner arrives."

Pallas looked stricken, but fear overcame his shame and soon Hallows could hear his heavy-footed departure upon the staircase. Emerging into the laneway, Pallas looked back only once, and then was gone.

Hallows realized that he was now truly alone; he thought through his options, all of which seemed desperate. He was, after all, just a rouge knight upon the board—they had coloured him blood red.

He could almost imagine himself seated at his small table, head slumped forward, arms cradled in a pool of blood, a shadow standing behind him; bishop takes knight.

No, not yet, he thought defiantly, *I'm still one move ahead of you—one move? Yes*, he decided, *I shall pass through Gienne and Salia on the way down—a drowning man will clutch at the blade of the knife.*

The piece of paper had lain for a time upon the table, but now Hallows crumpled it up and threw it through the grating into the fire; afterwards, he too went outside.

II

As Hallows made his way out into Fulgurator's Way via a side street, he noted a torn and tattered poster clinging tenaciously to one of the grimy walls.

THE THIRD KING IS DEAD, it screamed in blood-red lettering. ARE YOU CERTAIN? LOOK TO YOUR NEIGHBOURS AND FRIENDS. WRITE DOWN THE NAMES OF THE TWENTY PEOPLE CLOSEST TO YOU. FORGET NO-ONE. LATER YOU WILL NEED TO CONSULT YOUR LIST. REMEMBER: ARE YOU CERTAIN?

Hallows smiled wryly to himself, thinking that only days before he had been the unknown hero slaying the beast-king. Now he was a renegade. He fingered the small piece of paper in his pocket—the twenty names. In the circumstances, such a piece of paper could be especially dangerous. The guild would wish to reach him before somebody else did—yet all Sudima was on alert.

Sudima, city of secrets, city of eyes. All now appeared turned towards Hallows, or so he thought. Yet to get to the sectors of Gienne and Salia he must first pass through the ever-observant masses. Look to your windows indeed.

Would they dare strike him down in the street? Such was not usually the way of the whisper-guilds, but who could tell?

Hallows glanced nervously about him at the others: the teeming masses that filled Sudima's ever-expectant streets. Was there amongst them one who returned glances with a knowing smile? Or who turned away suddenly to exchange hidden contraband, a knife passed as one might pass a message? So easy to bump against another in the crowd, a mumbled apology then move on.

"The red one passes through the bazaar at Verpont . . . He heads east . . . east, always east . . ." So does the whisper trail pursue him.

Was it merely his imagination that made him think the turbaned man at the fish cart had said to his shadowy companion: "The tall one. See how he walks, so quickly?"

One move, just one.

Was it his imagination that constricted him thus, or was it something more? A man with the rags of a beggar pranced for a moment beside him like a hopeful dog, yet was there in his eyes not so much a pleading, but more a scrutiny. Perhaps his was the checklist: dark-haired, tall, angular. He fell behind, there were more whispered asides; someone standing within a doorway before was now gone. *To fetch the tea*, Hallows thought to himself sarcastically. *Ah yes, of course, the tea.*

Onwards! East, always east, through Albanois towards Gienne. Hallows fingered the small slip of paper in his pocket. The names!

Gienne, and to Executioners Square. You will walk its full circumference thrice. You will carry your jacket in your right hand for the first; wear it for the next two. Upon completion you will stand in the shadow beneath the Arch of the Martyrs. For five minutes will you wait. Should I come, you will know me by the name of the fourteenth martyred. I will know you not.

Hallows waited further back in the shadow than usual, for five minutes, then ten. He became jittery. He wasn't coming. A group of elderly men, resting upon benches and aligned around an extravagantly sculptured fountain leant their heads together conspiratorially. Occasionally they chuckled. Did he hear them mention something about the red one? He strained his ears to try to catch the gist of their conversation, and in so doing failed to notice the arrival.

"Good sir, wish you luck and manna, then you should seek protection."

A short, stout man holding a glass-topped tray, filled with gaudy trinkets, had sidled up to him.

"Within you will find protective tokens, talismans and amulets," he continued, warming to his pitch. "Each and any for three half pieces of silver. Or if you prefer, one full groat will purchase you three of these mystical and very ancient artefacts."

"I am interested in these martyrs depicted upon the Arch," Hallows said, feigning indifference. "Can you tell me something of their history?"

"Sir, sir, you ask the right man. I was named after the fourteenth martyr, Ponteroso, and I can show you artefacts very rare and valuable."

"Here?" Hallows asked, following a well-worn path.

"No, no, these artefacts are too rare to be brought to such a place. You must come with me; I will show you then."

"You will not show others these valuable artefacts," he said, grasping Ponteroso's arm in a firm grip.

"Not until sir has viewed and made his decision. Afterwards, of course, others too may wish to view."

"Such viewing comes at a price," Hallows whispered, as they left Executioners Square via another archway, out into a maze of back streets.

"Always!" agreed Ponteroso.

Thereafter they proceeded in silence.

III

THE RELIC SELLER'S HOUSE WAS hidden amongst a thousand similar dwellings in Gienne. However it had at its rear a large storeroom-cum-workhouse, wherein the so-called ancient artefacts were contained. They were no more than passably skilful fakery, many still in the early stages of construction. Ponteroso, of course, had other things on his mind.

"It is dangerous for you to come here," he said. "What possessed you?"

"I did only what I thought was right," Hallows replied, speaking of earlier happenings. "Am I now to be cast out for my devotion to the guild? Remember, Ponteroso, when I first came to you with details of the poet, you too were convinced of my choice."

"I believed you had delivered the Third King," the relic seller admitted. "All the omens were there. The assumption . . ." He shrugged his shoulders. "None of us are blameless."

"Yet it is I who will pay the ultimate price," Hallows reminded him. "Already the guild has its assassins upon my trail."

"All the more foolish then for coming here." Ponteroso sounded only slightly sympathetic. "You understand the way of things."

"Yet Tamarin . . ."

Ponteroso snorted in disgust. "Things were very different then, as you well know. Tamarin was a man accountable only to his conscience—he played by his own rules. The guild no longer harbours those who wish to kill for the pleasure of it. Besides, other guilds cater well enough for that."

Hallows shook his head. "If I am to be punished for this mistake, why should you not also accept responsibility? For the death was sanctioned; the guild chose me as the blade, the breaker of the invisible chains. It is you who are culpable."

Ponteroso only smiled, but it was as fake as his relics. "I am a true servant of the guild," he said evenly. "Should they wish my termination they needn't send an assassin; they know this. Besides, how could death have meaning to one such as I? Kill the right king, after all, and I shall unravel. Kill another and you too should fade. When you killed the poet you accepted this fact, that with his death your own passing could occur. The invisible chains that bind us to the masters must be broken. You tried and failed, now you too must pass into that other place. But you will be remembered—that, the guild promises you."

"Promises and lies," Hallows snapped. "How do I know that with the fall of the kings we shan't all fade, and that the world will end?"

"You speak as if a defender of the faith, "Ponteroso scolded.

"We take it as an act of faith," Hallows continued undaunted. "Yet how can we know?"

"We can't," Ponteroso agreed. "But we can study carefully the results of previous king's deaths."

"The lists," Hallows muttered.

"Yes, the lists, "Ponteroso agreed. "There are always a number of individuals who vanish completely; those whose link with the kings are strongest. But there are others who don't fade, but undergo changes. These are our lifelines, the reason for our optimism—they are released from the silken chains, but are strong enough in themselves to remain viable. Freedom!" Ponteroso was becoming excited by his own vision splendid. "Existence without tyranny."

"But perhaps these others are merely taken up by another king, "Hallows argued. "Saved from the abyss by another's belief. This too might explain the changes—a different view of the same object, variations on a theme."

Ponteroso was looking at him strangely now, almost as if seeing him for the first time. "You speak such things and yet you read Tamarin. You carry the knife."

"I don't know," Hallows admitted. "I don't know what to believe anymore."

"Then believe this." Ponteroso grasped his shoulder firmly. "We don't need the kings. Oh yes, we might have at the beginning. They were the creators back then, but now they are going one by one and the world continues because we wish it so. *We* are the new kings, each and every one of us! With the fall of each of the old kings, less and less of those named are lost; the dead hand that has held us is prised free one finger at a time. Eventually we shall be free of them altogether." Ponteroso's eyes gleamed. "Why, who knows, you might even be a king yourself. Have you ever thought of that?"

Hallows shivered. "Occasionally," he admitted. "And you?"

"Of course," Ponteroso said. "We all have that dream. And, after all, we may just be right. It is said that the aspect is never aware of its true potential, that the kings have learnt to camouflage their presence so well that they are no longer aware of themselves."

Ponteroso looked at him with undisguised curiosity. "So what will you do, eh? Kill me. Is that what you have come here to do?"

"I'm not sure," Hallows shrugged. "That might have been part of it, but there's something I feel compelled to do."

"And what is that?"

"I intend to reach Salia if I can before the bishop."

"The bishop?"

"The guild's assassin."

Ponteroso laughed. "You see yourself as a pawn in this game, then?"

Hallows didn't reply.

"Or perhaps you have a grander design?"

Hallows could almost see Ponteroso's mind ticking over.

"You are confused, uncertain of your status . . ." His eyes began to widen.

Hallows had picked up the cast of a broken statue.

*   *   *

"The red one through Gienne, moving east . . . a martyr dead, battered to death beneath the bridge . . ." So does the whisper trail pursue him.

IV

WHOSE SIDE WAS HE ON? Hallows wondered as he continued east. His surroundings were now little more than a blur. He had killed for one and now the other. He didn't know why he had killed Ponteroso, he had just known at that moment that he must.

The recognition—the way Ponteroso's eyes had suddenly widened, the flash of illumination. There had been no fear, not even when the casting had come down, only what? Revelation? Could that have been what he saw? Had Ponteroso truly thought him a king—the Third King even?

The speed of the collapse of his previous belief system had left Hallows struggling to retain any semblance of stability. *Perhaps I am simply going mad*, he decided. In the past he might have asked himself what Tamarin would do in this situation, but that now seemed somehow inappropriate. Yet he headed still for Salia, Tamarin's place of death. *Too late now for contingency plans*, he decided; his instincts had carried him this far, so he had best continue to Salia, and once there . . .

Someone stepped out in front of him from the shadow of a doorway. A halting hand was placed upon his breast—a figure, long-haired and shambling. His clothing suggested a bohemian bent, green eyes. Too late Hallows remembered the poet. The man embraced him for a moment, then stepped away. In a twinkling he had gone. Hallows felt faint and leant against the cool stones of a building for support. As he did this he studied the thing that had been pressed into his hand, and tried to assimilate the whispered message.

"To the red one, from a long friend of the half man; at Salia a king will die. Of those in waiting, one is lost, the other a madman . . ."

So it appeared that he was not alone after all. He still had his supporters in the city, though who they could be he had no idea.

The half man . . . a name as used by the whisper guilds, a code for someone important, a guildmaster perhaps. But not

124

of the Lords of Chaos, and then the mention of the king again. Hallows walked on, no less troubled for this latest encounter, and irritated at the ease at which he had been made to accept the knife. Hiding it beneath his coat, he decided that he was fed up with being used in this fashion. With the killing of Ponteroso he had striven to break free from the guild's control. In their way they were no different from the kings they chose to kill or defend, depending upon tradition or inclination, and he found that he no longer wanted any part of it.

As soon as he came upon a relatively quiet section of Sudima's streets, he simply dropped the knife and walked on. It clattered upon the cobble-stones and lay gleaming in the midday sunlight, the green jewels in the handle glittering. There it lay for a moment, studiously ignored by all those who passed, until finally a shadow loomed above it and a large hand reached down and collected it. The jewels in the handle turned a deep red.

*   *   *

Salia! Here it was that Tamarin had been struck down.

The daylight was in its last quarter as Hallows walked slowly out into the great square with its central statues and vast assemblage areas. Long ago, armies had been paraded here. Now there were only the departing merchants, packing up their portable wares upon small rickshaws and leaving before the onset of the curfew. The last of the afternoon crowd were also dispersing, as Hallows found himself momentarily moving against this tide, but soon he was beyond them and out into the middle of the square, where now only a few stragglers remained. He moved towards the coloured squares—the Salia mosaics.

A single figure was standing there already—waiting, tall and gaunt.

Stepping upon varying coloured pavings as if superstitiously avoiding cracks, Hallows advanced.

"Stepping upon three squares of the same colour in a row will bring you bad luck," the figure said with a chuckle, but without looking up from its contemplation of the patterns.

"It is written," it continued with less humour, "that when Tamarin died, his blood spattered across some of the coloured squares and formed the shape of the talons of an eagle." The figure looked up at Hallows, exposing its face, as it continued. "You seem surprised."

Hallows had stepped back.

"He will be here soon enough," the man with the dead poet's face said simply, and returned to his intense scrutiny of the mosaics.

"Who are you?" Hallows questioned.

"Did you know," the tall figure continued as if not hearing him, "that there are a million stories in these tiles? It just depends on what you're searching for. The answers are here." He waved an all-encompassing hand. "Here there are tragedies and epics, kings and gods and mortals. For example," he pointed out a particular group of squares, "what do you see there?"

"See? I see nothing," Hallows admitted. "Only . . ." he stopped in mid-stream.

Something had moved, coalesced; the pattern had taken on a shimmering quality. "I see a man," Hallows said. "In chains. He is struggling." Just as quickly, it was gone, the pattern of the squares had changed.

"I didn't see the man in chains," the tall figure said. "I saw instead a short man being struck with a cast. See here also," he pointed out another section of the mosaic. "Here I see a knife dropped, and here I see it retrieved by another." He stepped out across the vast expanse of coloured squares, here and there pointing out interesting features.

"Here are three kings," he said. "One whose reign is ending, another who is lost and a third insane. Here I see a city of vast towers shrouded in eternal darkness and here another city, yet the same—a city of whispers. And within this city a half man who knows himself not. Here I see a red prince destined to become a king. Do you not see these things?" the tall man asked again.

"I see them," Hallows agreed. "But not in the squares."

The tall man smiled. "It is enough that you see."

"At Salia a king will die!" Hallows repeated the earlier message. "Of those in waiting, one is lost, the other a madman."

"Lost no longer," the tall man replied. "And as for the other, alas naught is healed. You shouldn't have relinquished the knife."

"The bishop—the guild's assassin . . ." Hallows began.

"He may not yet know himself," the tall man encouraged. "You may still have the advantage."

"How so?"

"The squares! Tamarin once fell before the talons of the eagle; he may well fall there again."

V

THE SQUARE HAD EMPTIED NOW. Hallows and the tall man were alone. An eerie dusk was settling upon the city and a cold breeze plucked at their garments.

"He is here," the tall man said at last. He was not looking at the squares, but out across Salia towards one of the four great archways that fed people into the square—the same archway through which Hallows himself had entered. A dark figure now stood framed beneath its shadow—a lifetime's walking it seemed, from their own position near the centre of the Square.

Hallows noticed something he had missed before; all the great statues at the centre of Salia had vanished and now there were more squares—thousands of them—revealing more intricate designs. Hallows thought he saw a bear standing on its hind legs, something that might have been a dog except it had a lion's head . . . there was a warrior with a golden helm and another with a long-tipped spear. Here he thought he saw . . . he stopped, then stepped back in fear. He had been standing in a pool of blood, covering what? Talons!

Hallows realised that he had found the eagle. He turned to report this discovery to the tall man, but he was gone. *Back into the squares*, Hallows thought to himself.

A king stared back at him from an ivory throne. And then the squares seemed to reassemble themselves and the king was gone, and with him the blood. The eagle, however, remained.

Hallows remembered Tamarin and looked up to see the dark shape standing not twenty strides distant, the knife in his hand and his feet upon the tip of the warrior's spear.

Hallows stepped slightly forward and the talons began to move.

At the first pass the eagle's talons ripped the spearman's thin white cloak and drew blood The frantic reply with his weapon merely found thin air, as the eagle circled upwards, confident in its abilities to wear this opponent down.

The second pass was better timed, and part of the spearman's cheek and nose were rent terribly. His blood flowed freely now, spattering upon the mosaic of a dark figure with a red jewelled knife—the inset rubies were like perfectly formed droplets of blood.

Hallows stood watching his opponent, unable to move a muscle. Their eyes met and held each other; Tamarin, however, was showing the first signs that he was perhaps losing the battle. A jagged scar had magically appeared on his left cheek and part of his nose now looked badly cut. If these setbacks worried him he gave no sign of it, at least not outwardly.

At the third pass the eagle tore at the spearman's scalp, attempting to get the blood to flow into his eyes. But the spearman was sharper of reflex this time and the spear tip was embedded into the eagle's side, ripping at his tendons. As the eagle lifted away he felt a weakness in his right wing, that quickly unbalanced his flight and had him tumbling back to earth.

Hallows felt his right arm go numb, and realized that the eagle was in trouble. If he allowed it to die, what then? *The Grey Wastes*, he thought fearfully; better to be lost in the city.

The spearman stepped towards the fallen eagle. He lifted the bloodied spear.

But Hallows had stepped off the squares—the eagle had gone.

Immediately Hallows' wounds became more intense; his right arm hung uselessly by his side and his body was drenched in blood. The only consolation was that Tamarin too revealed the true extent of his injuries. Like two torn and beaten alley cats, they faced each other on a darkening stage. The cold wind continued to blow and now the first wisps of night fog began to form about them, further obscuring the patterns of the squares. One thing remained unobscured, however, and that was Tamarin's knife. The red jewels gleamed in the gloom, a reminder to Hallows of the perilous nature of his situation. He had forsaken the detached, almost distant conflict of the squares for something far more direct and potentially lethal. After all, he had no obvious weapon, unless . . .

He watched as Tamarin began to circle him, like a predator considering its prey. His movements were indeed cat-like, almost graceful, in a deadly sort of way.

"Come any closer, Tamarin, and I will be forced to destroy you," he called out with as much confidence as he could muster.

Tamarin only laughed and edged ever nearer.

"Watch your step, for I have set for you a trap!"

"You lie!" Tamarin spoke at last and his voice was harsh and pained. Hallows remembered his injuries.

"The squares await your trespass with the gift of death."

"You have forsaken the squares," Tamarin replied, undeterred. "They cannot help you now."

He was right, of course. Hallows had chosen his way, but he thought, nonetheless, of one square, one unlike any others. It was different only in one respect—Hallows was standing on it.

He thought of this square, forgetting about Tamarin, about the knife, about everything else. He focused upon it. After a little while he imagined it somewhere where there was nothing else—emptiness.

Afterwards he did not think of anything else for a long time—only the square. Eventually, when he decided to expand his horizons he did so a little at a time. He thought of a second square, similar to the first, and then a third . . . He thought of squares of different colours . . . Eventually a pattern began to emerge. He followed it.

He walked across the rose, and the spires, and the dragon; he walked through fields of blue flowers, and deserts full of ruined castles. He walked beside the old man with the flowing beard, and the staff of yew, and the lady with the golden hair. He dallied in the halls of stone, and saw the flames, and the sword renewed. He witnessed the opening of the gate, and last of all, he came to the man in chains and released him; afterwards he remembered no more.

* * *

Hallows woke with the morning; he was lying upon the squares and all his wounds had healed. He got slowly to his feet, remembering as best he could what had happened to him. There was no sign of Tamarin, and indeed the pattern was different. Everything seemed altered—he saw no eagle, no spearman. There were other things, however, and one of them immediately caught his eye: a king upon an ivory throne. His face was familiar—it was Tamarin. But this Tamarin was different somehow; there were no scars—but more than that—he seemed at peace. His face radiated calm acceptance, perhaps even the beginnings of wisdom. Inset into the high-backed part of his throne was a knife, blade pointed downwards, its green jewels glowing. Then the squares seemed to reassemble themselves; the king was gone and Hallows was alone again.

He stood for a time in the vast square, pondering what had occurred and wondering if it were still Salia that he was in, or some other as-yet-unnamed square. Whatever changes had come to pass, instinctively he knew that he would never find out what they were.

As Hallows walked slowly towards the nearest archway, he understood the one great unchanging truth; no matter what manner of place existed beyond the arches, he would discover it in a new guise.

The old would be set side and he would walk out from beneath that arch, a stranger once more, ever frightened and uncertain, a stranger once again lost in the city.

The Ghosts Of Aspect Retrieval

I

IF CALWIN WAS STILL A tall man with reddish hair and blue eyes, then he would be satisfied. His auto-rememberers tracked him with loving detail, from the curve of his cheek to the roll of his walk; there was a tick to his left eye, a suggestion of a smile should he speak. His clothing changed depending upon his position within the miracle shop; the rememberers absorbed this ancient joke, without understanding. Yet there was even then method in the madness, for the weapons changed too. As Calwin passed the storerooms and workshops of the lower level, he constantly expected to encounter the false aspects, ghosts of his recently remembered selves lingering, yet the transferences were as ever smooth; why he should be disappointed at this he couldn't say. The enemy for now was held at bay, Starholder's protective walls were unbreached, and no drifting tendrils of mist had entered to damage or change. Amongst many other marvels stood the Harvel and the Tollard—the mannequins. At Calwin's arrival the smaller shape raised its head and began to talk to itself in a slow and deliberate tone, as if confirming an earlier enquiry.

"A Calwin," the Harvel said, "I shall begin again at tenth."

It shut down and the head tilted slightly forward. The other figure remained totally silent, though Calwin sensed its eyes watching him. *A Calwin*, he thought to himself, pondering the Harvel's mutterings. *No more and no less—an abstract.*

"Hollow men," he asked them, not overly expecting an answer, "what do you dream? What do you spy?"

The Harvel remained dead. The Tollard however replied in a voice as bright and cheerful as the clown face, hidden for now by the gloom. "I see the crusade" it said. "I dream the man who marks himself thrice to signify the change. He follows not in the vanguard, but in the host."

"I have heard this tale," Calwin said to the Tollard. "I have heard all the tales."

It fell silent again. *Cleaver instructed it well,* he thought, *this tale spinner.* Yet now its repertoire seems limited—a carnival curiosity, a clown without an audience. Calwin decided to move on, feeling perhaps a trifle foolishly, that his very silence mocked its simple calling. *Let it rest in the dark,* he thought. *Let it no longer be pushed at and abused by ignorant crowds.*

He was leaving the storeroom when the voice comes again. *The Tollard,* he thought to himself, *sputtering like a dying candle flame.* Despite himself he thought of Cleaver, Cleaver the sharp-ghost, the madman lost within his own creation—the twisting house. Calwin thought of all these things, but not for long. Dwelling upon such things could be dangerous, especially here in the Uncertain Areas.

His auto-rememberers moved him smoothly onto the second level, while down below all now was silent.

* * *

The night was receding. Calwin dreamed, but in the Uncertain Areas even dreams could become reality. His auto-rememberers tracked reality and fortified it constantly—the other things flickered and died, merely phantoms of his imagination, brought to life and now to death upon the meshing of Starholder's colour banded killwire and the uncompromising efforts of the rememberers. Not for Calwin the life of final aspect. Starholder's last gift thus rejected, he had chosen instead the precarious existence of the sharp-ghost. There were others such as him, outcasts and loners scavenging and shadowalking, a dangerous and occasionally short-lived profession; Calwin, however, had lasted longer and been more successful than most. His miracle shop positioned strategically along Monserat Parade was the result of that extended run of good fortune. Yet there was little time for self-congratulation. Calwin often thought of inner Rimora—Starholder's realm—in terms of a small outcrop surrounded by a vast and terrible sea. The Uncertain Areas were its craggy cliff faces, assailed by a constant rolling breaker of mist, a place of strange and darkly dangerous things.

* * *

Calwin rose from his bed within a clearing in a verdant forest, the smells of the wood a constant and pleasant companion; above him stars winked. The night air was cool and crisp. As his feet touched the dry leaf-coated earth of the clearing there was a brief clear whistle, like that of a carefree woodsman wandering, axe upon shoulder, between the trees. At this, one of the auto-rememberers shut down and another clicked on; although, as ever, the transference was soundless.

Calwin stood beside his bed, dressed now in an orange saffron shirt and dark brown slacks. He momentarily shook his head at his continuing lack of dress sense, but moved quickly to where the killwire hung. It was like a sentient many-coloured snake; from its small domed eyelet, set within the ceiling, it could reach out to any part of the room, eliminating unwanted insubstantials, dream residues or more exotic and dangerous intruders. This night had been a quiet one, with the colour bands signalling only green to light blue and there being no obvious smell of dissolved personae. Insubstantials and other such ghostly fragments often left a smell similar to that of crushed almonds. Their passing at the hands of the killwire often left Calwin feeling remorse and a certain ambiguity as to the worth of Starholder's protection device, yet he hadn't been able to bring himself to wish for its removal. His fear of the nightmares lurking within the mists was always counter argument enough.

The auto-rememberers rediscovered the door and as he stepped through he carried a fire stave.

$$*\quad*\quad*$$

Calwin walked slowly between the exhibits in his display room, glancing about to reassure himself that all was as it should be. He walked to a shelf and picked up a cube of crystalline design, filled with semi-potential melt-mist, within which floating tendrils of mist stirred as if sediments about an undersea geyser. Calwin concentrated for a moment, attempting to envisage a simple form—a hand being raised, five fingered. The mist coalesced, its potential being brushed by his simple imaging; it began to react. Suddenly a dark hand pressed against the inner surface of the cube, squirming; momentarily it seemed real enough to reach out through the protective layer and grasp at him. Calwin smiled to himself enjoying the game, old though it was. He let his concentration lapse and the squirming hand collapsed back into its component parts. *Old ghosts*, he thought to himself wryly.

He walked to the door. It opened out onto Monserat Parade and the mists, always the mists. He shrugged to himself. Life in the Uncertain Areas . . .

His auto-rememberers provided him with the winterkill. He experienced the slight blurring of his senses that indicated its presence, as if a net of infinitely fine mesh had been placed about him; a pendant was suddenly warm against his chest. Such precautions were unavoidable.

The auto-rememberer rediscovered the door. He was greeted by a quiet, wide, flagstone-paved street, not shrouded today in mist, there being only a few isolated patches that hung like mini fog banks, only partially obscuring the other side. Several gargoyle-encrusted facades indicated the continued presence of the one who called himself Hetic. A fellow scavenger, licence holder and sharp-ghost, his doorway, or the outer part at least, was a snarling, salivating demon, and being very much still in evidence, Calwin decided that the melt-mists must have been negligible, if not nonexistent overnight—a good sign for potential customers venturing out from inner Rimora. If not for the chances of a successful shadowalk; the tides had been too weak. He would leave his scavenging to a more propitious moment, perhaps after a storm, when the outer chaos threatened to sweep them aside as mere barnacles clinging tenuously to Rimora's skin.

He ventured further out into the street, his eyes adjusting to the light, or lack of it—daylight in the Uncertain Areas was a grey-green impostor. Combine that with the ever-present mist and it always seemed to be late evening, a damp unpleasant one. He looked up at his own shop front, which in reality, if such a thing applied here, was really an unprepossessing establishment, a simple sign in red lettering upon a white background above the door. No gargoyles or statues; less trouble replacing, however, when the inevitable melt-mists erased it. *Monserat Parade*, he thought. There were other streets too, of course, however none had been in memory for as long, and so consequently couldn't claim the same sense of place, of being.

Calwin was about to re-enter the shop when he noticed upon the flagstones, down there in the half light, something that he had missed upon first inspection—dry curled up leaves, scattered as if blown upon the ghost wind from some distant transitory forest. He smiled to himself, thinking that perhaps there had been a night tide after all.

II

THE DAY'S FIRST, AND AS it transpired only visitor, was a short man with greying hair, tired eyes and a smile of perpetual resignation. He wore a fawn suit with a crimson handkerchief protruding above his pocket like a bloodstain. Calwin spotted him first in the crystal eye; he was making his way in from Avatar Crossing. Calwin watched him as he approached through the mist, hastening along that long, lonely stretch of the first remembered way, as it tracked ever inwards, not snaking through the mists but running proudly straight, a singular memory in an uncertain land. Calwin studied the man's face for a moment, centring it within the crystal eye and calling upon a close-up. This was no sharp-ghost, that was for certain! Calwin knew each and every member of their small and now increasingly isolated community; besides, the wrinkles and thinning hair betrayed him as a final aspect. His blue eyes were humorously aware of the invisible but minute observation he was undergoing, and not just from Calwin. *Who are you my friend?* Calwin wondered to himself. *Sharp-ghost or final aspect?* And if he was a final aspect, which seemed the only logical explanation, then what the deuce was he doing approaching Calwin's construct from the direction of the outer chaos? He would soon find out, Calwin realised, because the man's footsteps were leading him inevitably towards the miracle shop. That is until he halted upon the very brink.

The auto-rememberer rediscovered the door, and the grey man stepped within.

* * *

"Such a show of force is unnecessary," the grey man said, smiling in his tired way. "I am of no danger to you."

Calwin's auto-rememberers remained constant. "This is merely a warning," the Calwin said. "I am capable of many aspects; with which one you deal depends largely upon your own actions. Another aspect will soon appear and greet you in more traditional form; I hope it will be of assistance. Remember, you have been warned."

The auto-rememberers moved smoothly between aspects, and Calwin stood behind his counter.

"You must excuse my show of force; regrettable as it may seem, there are times when such aspects fulfil a purpose."

"Certainly," the grey man said, acknowledging Calwin's presence with a slight tilt of the head. "Yet remembering machines have their limitations also."

"Undoubtedly," Calwin agreed, "but here in the Uncertain Areas it is an adaptation that favours us."

"Adaptation," the grey man said. "We all must adapt or die, must we not?"

Calwin nodded. The grey man was studying his shelves; they were packed with semi-potential melt-mist, cocooned in crystalline containers of all shapes and sizes. There were cubes and spheres, all intricately designed and produced to enhance their interior mysteries.

"No two the same," Calwin said, as if warming to a pitch. "The mist itself has many interesting properties, and can be made to form primitive approximations of almost anything you can imagine. Magic dust, I once heard one of my customers describe it. The very nature that allows it to break things down also allows those like Starholder, those with the talent to build, to create. "Unfortunately," he noted, "we sharp-ghosts are reduced to mere collection, deflection and containment. Such is our lot." He sighed.

"And should I wish to purchase such an object?" the grey man asked. "The payment . . . ?"

"Pattern . . . !" Calwin said, interrupting him. "It is always so."

"With sharpers, yes," the grey man agreed. He moved along the shelves studying the various distillations of an eternity of decay.

"How much pattern for these?" he asked, waving an all encompassing hand above the stock.

"Some for one," Calwin replied. "Some for two. The most expensive for four."

"Four?" The grey man raised an eyebrow.

"I do get large groups at times," Calwin said. "They are usually happy to supply payment; it is quite something to later tell their friends in Rimora. Not only did I venture out into the Uncertain Areas, but I even supplied pattern to a sharp-ghost—a kind of immortality."

The grey man laughed. "I hadn't thought of it like that."

"You have given pattern?"

"Once, yes, but not to a sharper."

This response puzzled Calwin. Pattern could only be taken from the same final aspect every seven years or so; even though pattern could be given freely to more than one sharp-ghost, continued exposure tended to age them prematurely.

The grey man was watching him closely, awaiting a response. Calwin decided not to disappoint him.

"You have the advantage over me final aspect. How can pattern be given if not to a sharp-ghost, a sharper as you term us?"

"I am not like other final aspects."

"That I had already deduced," Calwin said.

"You wonder, no doubt, how it is that I came to you from the direction of the mists?"

"I wonder many things," Calwin said, "and that is chief amongst them."

"I am what some of a more poetic bent might describe as a pale light cast by Starholder."

"I should have seen his hand in this." Calwin sighed, sensing he was about to be involved in something—probably something dangerous.

"Why has Starholder sent you to me?" he asked. Then, before the final aspect could reply, he held up his hand and added, "No, don't tell me. I am about to render invaluable assistance in recompense for unspecified past favours. Am I correct?"

"Almost word for word." The grey man nodded, smiling. "You are something of a favourite, apparently," he added.

"There are undeniable advantages in such a position," Calwin agreed. "But I feel this is not going to be one of them."

"You will be well recompensed for your assistance," the final aspect offered.

"You will give pattern then?" Calwin asked.

"No, I cannot," the grey man replied. "With Starholder I didn't give Pattern, but receive."

"I don't understand."

"Neither really do I."

There was silence for a moment, as the consequence of the grey man's words sank in. "Pattern will be provided by twelve upon completion of our task," he said at last.

"Twelve, you say?"

The grey man nodded.

"On the surface it seems generous," Calwin conceded.

"This task you speak of," he began, measuring his words, "it concerns my once colleague, Cleaver, does it not?"

"No. No," Calwin waved him silent, "let me continue, I have received no temporal correspondence, but I have dreamed and thought of little else."

"Cleaver," the grey man confirmed. "The way has been prepared."

"The way . . . ?" Calwin questioned.

"Surely you haven't forgotten so soon?" It sounded like Starholder himself, scolding him through an intermediary. "Remember the hand that was opened, the hand that was given access to Rimora, the hand that then closed and withdrew, taking with it much that was prized—sharper treachery."

"The twisting house," Calwin said, catching on. "Cleaver's carnival."

There was an edge to the final aspect's words, a personal dimension. "I am sorry for your loss," Calwin said, realizing what that was and acknowledging the grey man. "Final aspect must be terrible at such a time?"

The grey man was silent for a moment, as if considering the apology. "My wife and son," he said at last. "At first I blamed all sharpers . . ." His voice trailed away.

"We have paid for Cleaver's crime," Calwin reminded him. "Further exile, for all of us, even those who you might term favourites." He smiled weakly.

"You are hero and villain in equal parts," the grey man said, seemingly speaking for all the residents of the Uncertain Areas.

"Then what can this one poor, flawed sharper do to tilt those scales?" Calwin offered.

"The doorway by which Cleaver insidiously introduced himself into our midst," the grey man began, "the doorway by which he stole that which was not his—Cleaver's twisting house. With the help of Starholder's pattern I have recreated it."

"You have the door," Calwin said, "and now what?"

"The key!" the grey man exclaimed." The Tollard, Cleaver's clown; I know you possess it."

"I have the clown," Calwin agreed.

"You see," the grey man said, finally revealing the workings of a complex and previously hidden plan, "Starholder did not give up on the lost ones so easily."

"I am Calwin," the sharp-ghost said. "And you?"

"I am Randt."

"Good," Calwin said. "Now we had best go and get the clown; no doubt it too has a story to tell."

III

LEAVING THE MIRACLE SHOP, CALWIN and Randt, with the Tollard in tow, prepared to walk through the inevitable clinging mist back up Monserat Parade, toward the outer chaos. Calwin, upon first setting foot out of his construct, checked that his personal rememberers, his aspect retrieval system, was operating at maximum efficiency. As Randt watched with something approaching amusement, Calwin appeared, and then reappeared, each time, as before, his attire and weaponry altered with each passing aspect. At last he settled upon his travelling attire—a comfortable sweater, long trousers, thick boots and a staff with a crystalline head, melt-mist curling mysteriously within.

"All satisfactory," he said at last, as if running some well-practised check list through his head.

"Ready?" Randt said, seemingly impatient to get started.

"Almost," Calwin said, "but first . . ."

He struck the staff against the now smooth, door less exterior. Immediately a small spark seemed to pass from the wall into the head—a wall of blue fire rose up and blanketed the construct.

"Disruption field," Calwin said, "in case I don't return before the tides."

"But isn't it automatic?" Randt questioned.

"Yes, but it also causes the mists to attempt something similar." A small blue flame now emanated from the head of the staff, casting them in an intimate glow.

He turned and looked back down Monserat Parade, towards where the first remembered road, flagstone-paved and wide, passed through the ever-present and obscuring mist, to reach eventually the beginnings of an even greater disruption field; this was Rimora's outer skin, Starholder's first defence against that which they battled nightly. Before reaching this beginning, however, it passed by several other constructs, including one other 'shop,' and of course the Collection Centre. Pressed up against Rimora's bulk, the Collection Grading and Pattern Distribution Centre, as it was officially known, protruded both without and within, spanning both worlds. The centre of life in the Uncertain Areas, all sharpers relied upon its pattern distribution as much as they relied upon their disruption fields. Every shadowalker's dream was to find potential; out there in the mists, there were places where things that had once existed could exist again, for a time, places where the mists were especially pure. Here the mixtures brought forth the mists' Potential. By shadowalking, sharp-ghosts could find all manner of these places, but it was the mist itself they most desired, that most pure distillation. Once found, it would be collected and returned to the Uncertain Areas, where it would be sold through the Collection Centre to Starholder himself—the source of his power. In return they did receive pattern, life for life. Calwin, of course, had a greater interest in this than most; the slightly less pure form, rejected in grading, went to those licensed by Starholder such as Calwin and Hetic, who on-sold it to visiting final aspects as keepsakes, earning extra pattern for their troubles.

As they turned to leave Calwin wondered what Hetic, his neighbour, sometimes friend and inevitably, considering their adjacent proximity, competitor for custom, was making of all of this. The salivating demon, contained upon each side by gargoyle-like statues, marked the entrance to his shop come construct—Blackwraith's Emporium. Hetic believed the best chance of success came in contrast.

No doubt he was at this moment centring them within his crystal eye, and clicking his teeth with his tongue in that way he had. At least he would be without competition for a time, Calwin thought. As they settled into stride, following Monserat Parade's determined progress through the mists, Calwin noted that the day, or at least the day as it was in the Uncertain Areas, was clear, though curling tendrils of melt-mist still licked at them as they passed. Melt-mist in its passive form floated about them like cloudlets. On either side of the road it was a thick greenish pea soup, welling and puckering. The light it emitted was something that shouldn't have been called light; it was a travesty. *Ghosts again*, Calwin thought to himself, *the mists' response to an eternity of dissolved memories*. Always there was day and night. The mist couldn't give clear blue skies and puffy white clouds, at least not consistently; it couldn't give hot bright suns, but it could give something that was different from night, or as different as it could manage. *Thank heavens for that, at least*, he thought . . .

Safely haloed in their ghostly blue shawl, they progressed up Monserat Parade, three small figures upon a road to nowhere, surrounded by mist.

They passed more constructs, disruption fields intact, sizzling evilly as they dissolved intruding melt-mists that brushed up against them. It was this that often disappointed the tourists, Calwin thought to himself. They expected the Uncertain Areas to be full of wonders, yet it was mostly just this, blue sizzling walls and green cloying mist. Only the shops, Calwin's and the others, generally lived up to expectation.

"Remember," he always told them, "you only see the Uncertain Areas during what passes here for day. When the night tides come, there is no point in having overly ornate decoration; the mists will simply dissolve it away. Here simplicity is survival. Sometimes even disruption fields can fail. Most of we sharpers, as you term us, are only ever a heartbeat away from disaster; it is not a game for us."

Not a game indeed.

Another construct passed, another disruption field, and now looming out of the melt-mist was the first great auto-rememberer station, the original rememberer; its four faces traced the intersection of Monserat Parade with Avatar Crossing. Randt and Calwin slowed as they neared this intersection. Starholder's stony visage stared down at them approvingly; behind his eyes there was once and forever Monserat Parade. Here even the melt-mist seemed cowed.

"Straight ahead . . . ?" Calwin asked.

Randt nodded. "A long way yet."

As they continued past the Starholder totem, Calwin had no doubts that whatever happened to the Uncertain Areas, or indeed to Rimora itself, these streets would remain remembered forever. Old things would come to their end, new things would appear, grow, fail and cease. The mists would always dissolve, time itself might be lost, complicated things become untenable, but in its simplicity . . . He let this final thought hang.

As they shuffled forward, passing the occasional fire-blue construct wall, Calwin noticed the mists altering subtly; they were entering a patch replete with possibilities. A forming of things was occurring, ghostly transitions, limbs partially formed like knobbly tree trunks, gnarled and old, then breaking apart like waves crashing against rocks that might have been heads, bald, smooth and dark, that became teeth-sharp and regular, or the protruding forms of turrets.

Unrealized potential . . . Calwin thought to himself. *Just the mist dreaming in its most simple form.*

On the way itself the mist was much more fragmented, though what there was tended to want to cling to their bodies. They passed through it as if ice-breakers, through banks that parted and fell away, only to reform once they had passed.

Ahead new constructs loomed. 'Tavon's Safe House,' sizzled and crackled fiery letters, the disruption field cleverly jumping and discharging. Messages of welcome brought to life by the dissipation of the mist. Inside final aspects could find such things as Calwin's ilk had been forgiven long before. Upon the other side Forlston's entrance greeted the newcomer, with its twin beakers, those twice the size of a normal man. Inside a very special concoction of melt-mist swirled—potential, almost 100% pure, still the only known case of Starholder gifting away such a thing. *Why Forlston?* he wondered, not for the first time professional jealousy getting the better of him. *Provided in recompense for unspecified past favours*, a small voice within answered, and he could but smile. As they passed close by, the potential within the beakers began to twist and curl, beginning to approximate their forms, even this briefest most inconsequential of contact enough to bring it to life.

Leaving this last bastion of light in the darkness behind, they now passed beyond the point where final aspects were compelled by law to turn back, heading now deeper out into a world of mist and uncertainty.

IV

So far they had travelled in silence, but now Calwin decided to question his taciturn companion. "This construct," he began, "why so far out?"

They were approaching the second auto-rememberer station, the one that traced Fallstaff Crossing as it intersected with their intended route.

"Safety," Randt said simply.

"Safety . . . ?" Calwin replied, attempting to keep the sarcasm from his voice. "You go deeper out into the melt-mists, out into this." He waved a hand at the surrounding mists, which, if anything, seemed to have thickened. "For safety?"

"Of course," Randt replied.

"There are many who would call you crazy."

"Then they would be unwise," he said evenly. "I am well aware of what it is I carry. Others are not, and Starholder would have it remain that way."

"Ah, the reverse pattern," Calwin said in sudden realization. Then he shook his head in further understanding. "You think so little of we sharpers. Indeed, Starholder should think so little." His annoyance was evident.

"Precautions are necessary," Randt said simply. "The less that know . . ."

"But pattern . . . none would force themselves."

"Can you be sure of that?" Randt replied. "Can you speak for all?"

Calwin hesitated.

It was enough for the final aspect, who turned away, point seemingly made.

Pattern vampires, Calwin thought unhappily. Such things had been known to happen, but it was rare, and those who had resorted to such low means were quickly dealt with—a one way trip to the Grey Wastes, leaving an empty construct, disruption field retracted, for the mists.

They were so far out now, almost as far as the Sternguard Crossing, and hadn't seen a construct for many minutes. The sharpers tended to cluster together closer to Rimora, as if moths afraid to venture too far from the light.

"When we reach the Sternguard Crossing," Randt said, "we shall turn to the left and follow it into nearly its farthest remembering, before the way begins to peter out, to lose itself in the outer chaos."

Calwin nodded.

When reached, that final rememberer station, the third, towered above them in the mist; ahead of them, Monserat Parade continued gamely, indomitably, yet somehow hopelessly, outward.

They stopped for a moment, contemplating this point of intersection. There was something frightening about this, the last remembered road, something lost.

"One day," Calwin said, attempting to leaven the sense of dread, "Starholder will add a further remembering post somewhere out there, extending the Uncertain Areas by a further crossing, and then another and another. In time he hopes to build up a hundred remembered streets."

"World building," Randt agreed, "what he is good at, but it will not be easy; here the melt-mist is still king."

Leaving the final remembered stretch of Monserat Parade, to meet its inevitable demise out there in the mists, they turned and followed the progress of Sternguard Crossing.

This was so far out of the way, Calwin thought; it was indeed unlikely that other sharpers would ever stumble upon it. Shadowalkers needed to travel no further than their own construct to enter the outer chaos; they just needed the knack, the talent.

Now at last Randt's construct came into view, it's disruption field shimmering. "Home at last," he quipped.

They halted on the brink, Randt standing still and allowing his construct's pattern recognition to work its arcane magic upon him. The disruption field collapsed—his auto-rememberers rediscovered the door. They stepped inside—the Tollard the last to enter, obediently three steps behind.

Calwin, feeling like a man holding an opened umbrella indoors, altered his aspect. The blue glowing staff vanished, and he now stood in the midst of Randt's construct in his saffron shirt, a seamless transition.

Randt's construct was a simple affair, a single room with several comfortable chairs, a bookshelf with several volumes and in the corner an unmade bed, the construct of one with little spare time to enjoy. Twin lamps set back in alcoves gave off a green glow, that was quietly changing to red even as Calwin watched. No sign of food or drink, he noted. He cast about for the rememberer stations; there were only half a dozen of them and those reasonably primitive. Originally portable, he decided.

Yet there was a deeper level to this, he realized, a multi-layered construct. Randt, who seemed to be reading Calwin's musings, just as Calwin was scouting his rememberers, spoke up and said, "The reconstructed twisting house is deeper within." He moved to the far wall.

An auto-rememberer rediscovered a corridor and Randt signalled for Calwin to follow. More stations along the corridor—rooms partitioned off, things contained. Randt stopped in front of one, seemingly uncertain about his next action. "Starholder gave me licence," he began, "for this reverse pattern as you have termed it; I am, as far as I know, the first to be so gifted. Remember we spoke of adaptation earlier; well perhaps I am to be the first of many. Yet if I am to be what you might call a template, then he must be able to trust me."

"Truly he must," Calwin replied, "for him to give you such advantages."

"Yet I have done something that might endanger that trust."

Calwin instinctively understood what that was.

"I was lonely you see," Randt explained, "and still I dream, but they are only things of the mist, less even than sharpers; no insult intended."

"None taken," Calwin assured him.

"But I cannot bring myself to cast them out, though I know that eventually I must."

"And I . . . ?" Calwin asked.

"I don't know," Randt admitted, "It is just better that you know; I feel that."

Calwin acknowledged this with a tilt of the head, but felt a sense of unease growing. *There are consequences*, he thought. *There are always consequences in knowing.*

They continued down the corridor. A blank wall faced them, but not for long—Cleaver's reconstructed twisting house.

V

To CALWIN WHO HAD SEEN the original, the similarity was uncanny. At least from the outside, here was the same crazy wizard's castle, with all those strange jutting angles and crazily positioned towers. The fake windows were there as well, with their eerie painted-on shadows, which still somehow seemed to move within, like the silhouettes of humpbacked witches, mounted knights and bearded wizards. The doorway was open, compressed outwards as if wider in the middle than at either end; it conveyed a sense of weight bearing down, or perhaps it was approximating a mouth.

"Remarkable," Calwin said. "Cleaver's twisting house lives."

"Not yet." Randt smiled sadly. "But when the clown enters, perhaps then."

"Why the clown . . . ?"

"Starholder retrieved it, gifted it to you; he called it the gatekeeper. He indicated that I should acquire it from you, once I had built the replica construct, and now that we are here, he also warned me to come prepared."

"Hence my presence," Calwin said. He acknowledged to himself his readiness—within him his aspect retrieval System shuffled.

"Time to move," he said. "We have waited long enough. Hollow man," he said to the Tollard, "enter the twisting house." This the Tollard did, sharp-ghost and final aspect close behind.

* * *

Three figures were standing upon a paved road beneath a beating sun; the road was surrounded by forest. There were broken statues every thirty metres or so, dotted along the road— pathway guardians. Calwin's concentration had wavered away from his companions for a moment, so he hadn't sensed the change, but as always he was ready to react. The gatekeeper, a tall golden-helmed figure cloaked in chain mail, lunged at him.

No normal sword . . .

As his rememberers absented him, he tried to interpret its design and choose a suitable riposte.

A hot sword . . . It would cut through the winterkill, so full body armour and a fire stave; he would fight fire with fire.

He reappeared.

Stave against sword . . . they clashed. Calwin was forced back, his armour charred. He noticed Randt watching from the side. *Wish me luck*, he thought, as he moved in close once more.

The gatekeeper circled to the right, its eyes unnaturally bright beneath its helm, the hot sword humming. Calwin didn't follow, but instead allowed himself to begin a feint in the opposite direction, the gap between them widening as if a piece of elastic; soon enough it would bring them rushing together. But it was Calwin with the longer reach; his weapon, though not as powerful, could strike at a greater range. He darted forward, strike and retreat . . . A ragged, charred hole had appeared in the gatekeepers chain mail, but it seemed unconcerned, merely recoiling slightly as if stung. This wasn't going to be easy, Calwin realized; the gatekeeper was obviously some form of mannequin left behind by Cleaver, as a sort of welcoming present for anyone opening the gate. *How typically magnanimous of him*, Calwin thought, simultaneously telling himself not to let the gatekeeper get side-on to him—the fear of the hot sword slicing his stave in two upmost in his thoughts. While at distance, the advantage was with him.

Calwin feinted to advance once more, but held his position; the gatekeeper toppled forward, almost overbalancing. Calwin, sensing his chance, aimed the point of his stave at a place between the gatekeeper's eyes. Even as he began this killing thrust, however, he knew it to be his doom; the hot sword's upward momentum was clearly greater and they were destined to meet at an angle that could only result in one thing—Calwin's stave was severed in two from below. The point, deflected somewhat, embedded itself harmlessly in the gatekeeper's helm, where it quivered like an arrow. Calwin, letting go of the stave, stumbled back, knowing a return to aspect-retrieval was called for. He was given no such opportunity, as the gatekeeper now turned its attention away from Calwin and stepped instead towards Randt. He had little choice. He threw himself forward.

Within him a dozen aspects shuffled . . .

As he grasped the mannequin in an enveloping hold, as it began to turn, he felt the familiar wave of despair wash over him.

The hot sword entered him.

It brought sharp pain, and then came the merciful darkness. Aspect-retrieval recaptured him.

Pattern flared . . . gone!

Aspect-retrieval opened once in that other place, then closed off.

A Calwin . . .

* * *

Randt had taken the opportunity to retreat to the edge of the path, while the gatekeeper was momentarily pulled into that other place, its form distorted and stretched, the top half elongated and blurred, while its legs and torso remained seemingly unaffected. The experience had either merely disconcerted it, or damaged it irrevocably. It seemed likely to have been the latter, as it fell over and began to jerk, as if a malfunctioning machine.

Calwin was suddenly back, standing upon the path in his saffron shirt.

"It died a little too," he said simply.

* * *

"What do we do now?" Randt asked.

The gatekeeper's spasms had become more and more infrequent, and Calwin was now standing rock-still, as if absorbing electrical waves from the air. "I'm just scouting the stations," he said. "There are auto-rememberers everywhere. There must be hundreds of them."

"The twisting house was the largest construct ever," Randt agreed, "large enough to contain over two hundred people in various fantasy environs, when Cleaver retracted it."

"There are similar devices to this gatekeeper," Calwin said, "a dragon, a witch, several wizards and others. Most now seem inactive, but no doubt will be moved against us if and when we are discovered."

"So you don't think we have been?"

"No," Calwin said, "the gatekeeper was a sort of automated respond and destroy relic, linked to the clown mannequin."

"Sort of interior and exterior sections of a lock . . . ?"

"Possibly," Calwin said, pondering for a moment. "Yes, I think you have hit upon it."

"So Cleaver is in for something of a surprise then," Randt exclaimed.

Calwin didn't comment for a moment, and when he did he changed the subject. "To find Cleaver we must follow the auto-rememberer trail to where most converge, which seems to be upon a hill about four miles distant from here. If you want to find a spider, look to the centre of its web."

"A long walk ahead of us then . . . ?"

"I'm afraid so."

* * *

Often did he sit here and consider his works—alone—but not today.

At first the two small figures registered barely a second thought; he let his mind reach out . . . An auto-rememberer!

He sat bolt upright.

Impossible . . .

But there it was again.

The two figures drew nearer. He rose from his throne, not in greeting but in challenge. "Who comes memorised into my presence?"

"I do," Calwin said, close enough to be recognized. They halted before him. Cleaver studied them for a moment. He was a large man with jet black hair and a round, not unpleasant face, but there was a certain something about his eyes, which, unlike most sharpers, were green; but there was a tendency for them to dart about as if not wishing to be pinned down, a certain furtiveness. He wore a cloak of grey with the faintest hints of gold, like the ghosts of lions glimpsed momentarily in burnt underbrush.

"The shopkeeper," he said at last, nodding to himself as if confirming a memory. "What brings you so far from your apron and counter, Calwin?"

"Our mutual friend wants returned something you once stole from him," Calwin said.

"You were always Starholder's creature." Cleaver snorted derisively. "It appears you remain so."

"Guilty as charged," Calwin replied, "though you too were given advantages. What you did with them has damaged us all."

Cleaver smiled. "All sharpers together, eh? Group solidarity and all that?" His face suddenly hardened. "The Uncertain Areas are an experiment doomed to failure. Starholder uses you all, and now he sentences you to many deaths here in my construct. I have been expecting you, Calwin, or someone like you—did you really think I wouldn't? So what say I give you access to my twisting house, the full guided tour?" He chuckled. "Will you take that challenge?"

His voice suddenly echoed, as his rememberers carried him away on invisible wings.

Randt and Calwin were left alone.

"He bolts like a coward." Randt seemed surprised.

"But he gives me a chance to follow."

"How do you mean?"

"He has de-customized some of the rememberers."

"I still don't understand?"

"They are no longer Cleaver specific; they will allow another sharper to be memorised down the line. The catch is, it will be to places of his choice."

"But he will have prepared well for this eventuality. He will have laid traps."

"Almost certainly . . ."

"Then why?"

"To give us time to find his weak point."

"If he has one . . ."

"There's always a weak point," Calwin said. "All we must do is find it. I must . . ."

Suddenly Randt saw Calwin's form vanish, return and vanish again, his aspects revealed one after another, as if a great hand were shuffling him as a deck of cards. The auto-rememberer, Randt realized—uplifting him, or attempting to.

Calwin vanished at last. The rememberers bore him away into Cleaver's construct, as a struggling hare in the talons of an eagle.

VI

DARKNESS. CALWIN WONDERED IF HE was in the Grey Wastes. He ran through his options, choosing the winterkill; the pendant should have been warm against his chest—nothing! He tried again. Eventually it came—the darkness became prismatic. Something that had been reaching out for him screamed in pain and retreated. In the darkness he waited, letting the winterkill barrier expand further.

His aspect-retrieval system was not well integrated into this new master memory, as its response was sluggish. When he tried to cause it to change aspects again, there was a momentary sticking or fazing; he nearly experienced a ghost field, his remembered selves merging. Cleaver's auto-rememberer was going to be a problem, he realized. His blue-staffed version eventually arrived.

Calwin was in what appeared to be a dungeon. The winterkill barrier had done its work—Cleaver's weapon and part of his bloodied hand were contained in the block of ice. He had been forced to depart wounded; had he not, then an entire aspect would have been contained in that block. Calwin, despite his inbuilt disadvantage, had drawn first blood, literally. Still, Cleaver's auto-rememberer was like a dead hand upon his aspect-retrieval system's response time, and a slow response time could equate to death. He had been lucky this first time.

He had a sudden thought and approached the block of ice. He needed a new aspect, one with an axe.

Placing the staff upon the block of ice, he tried for one.

The transference was tortuous; for a moment it appeared he wouldn't be retrieved at all, but eventually he stood in light chain mail with his weapon of choice. He immediately hacked into the block of ice, and retrieved not Cleaver's weapon but his fingers. He had no time to ponder this further, as his aspect-retrieval system was suddenly and urgently overridden, Cleaver switching him to a new focal point. He had time to place the bloodied fingers in a side pocket, before the world changed.

* * *

They were in a clearing in the forest, Calwin standing in one corner, Cleaver directly opposite him.

"You were a fool to come here," Cleaver said.

"How's the hand?" Calwin just said in reply. He thought he detected a flicker of what . . . uncertainty; perhaps even fear upon the face of the other sharper, but then it was just as quickly gone.

"Die then, shopkeeper," he said dismissively.

Calwin realized too late that Cleaver was floating marginally above the ground—the field flicked on and a Calwin did die—again.

* * *

Afterwards, Cleaver moved on to his next focal point.

A Calwin hung for a time over the clearing, a bizarre crucifix. An aspect-retrieval pattern passed, but the auto-rememberer at first refused to retrieve. Somewhere within there was recognition.

Calwin now floated high above the clearing in his saffron shirt, a bloodied finger in his hand.

* * *

He was everywhere and nowhere.

He was in the keep of a castle, in the main street of a town, at the side of the baker, amongst those who worked the fields; he was beside a river and in the deepest forest. He spoke with children, he frightened the sheep and disturbed the geese—he came not for pattern but with hope, and when he had gone there were those who could almost believe again. There was about to come a change.

Everywhere he went he left the same message, and then at last he came to Randt.

"The bird is on the wing," Calwin said.

* * *

Randt smiled in some relief. "I thought you dead many times by now."

"Just the once," Calwin admitted, "and that a misjudgement."

"What about our sharper friend?"

"He will soon be active," Calwin warned.

"But how is it that you are able to return here? I thought Cleaver to be in control of the rememberers."

"He was, but I have divined upon the source of our salvation."

"And what may that be?" Randt asked.

"Pattern recognition," Calwin offered.

"What?"

"Later," Calwin assured him, "but now you must make for the town; I have asked for all the lost ones to gather there. We must move swiftly; I will do my best to hold him." He vanished again.

* * *

Calwin's auto-rememberer—yes, he felt it to be truly his now—moved him to a space in the town square; people were already beginning to gather there. Cleaver had sent one of his servants, a wizard, much like the gatekeeper, to regain control; it had begun to threaten them. When Calwin appeared, they cheered.

He stood; it must have seemed to them, completely unarmed. But even as the wizard, tall and in blue robes, carrying some form of lightning discharger, began to approach him, Calwin dug deeper, scouting the stations to find the connections that were allowing Cleaver to activate it.

Priority! He thought.

It halted.

He grinned. Now he tried to get it to back off.

No result . . . a stalemate.

He shrugged. Good enough.

He waited . . . the crowd began to grow. Finally he came— Cleaver appeared in the centre of the square. He had obviously tooled up ready for battle; he was carrying a white shield and a hot sword. He had light body armour and there were three or four other weapons at his belt.

He had no aspect-retrieval system; Calwin realized almost immediately; he needed to carry all his cards physically into battle. He had an entire construct to move about in, yet he could only appear one aspect at a time; Calwin stored this away in his memory—he may well have an advantage.

Cleaver advanced, hot sword extended. Calwin stepped to the side, wondering how to combat this gambit. He was down two aspects, and what remained didn't measure up to the firepower lined up against him; the winterkill, his ace in the pack, would be ineffective against a hot sword, and he had lost his fire stave to the Gatekeeper. His remaining offensive aspects, axe and sword, would be hopelessly outgunned. He backed away, trying to think on his feet.

He reached out . . . the blue wizard, unnoticed by Cleaver, had returned to life and begun to move towards him.

Simple command structure, Calwin thought, *the weapon* . . . The blue wizard lifted its arm to aim. The crowd drew in their breaths. Cleaver, alerted by this, vanished.

Calwin cursed inwardly and the blue wizard toppled over, jerking.

Priority! He thought, but it was too late.

Cleaver returned, still armed to the teeth and now definitely in the ascendancy, but he was still being cautious.

Calwin prepared to flee, but he couldn't stop himself thinking of all the people watching him; he, Calwin the sharper, was their champion. He couldn't run, not this time. His aspect-retrieval system provided the Calwin with a sword.

He stepped forward.

* * *

Salvation came from an unexpected source, someone pushing themselves through the crowd and out into the battle circle, a singular figure in a fawn suit with a blood red pocket handkerchief—Randt.

Calwin saw his chance, probably his last. "The blue wizard," he called out to the final aspect, "get its staff."

Randt turned to where the wizard lay.

"Quickly," Calwin called.

Cleaver also sensed the danger and turned.

Randt darted forward and prized the staff free; he lifted it in time to see Cleaver almost upon him—he found the control.

An arc of blue fire caught the sharper full in the chest and engulfed his form; he crackled like a disruption field, and then he was gone.

Randt lowered the staff, white-faced but exultant, the crowd cheering. Calwin motioned for Randt to hand him the weapon. "Time to get them out," he said.

"I must find my family first."

"Make it double quick," Calwin said, "and then lead them all back to where we came in."

"What about you?"

"I don't know how many charges this thing holds," he admitted, "but when you're through I'm going to destroy the gateway behind us."

"That won't hold him," Randt said. "He will just shadowalk."

"I don't think so," Calwin replied, "not without aspect-retrieval."

"Really . . ."

Calwin nodded. "I'm going to trap him to this construct, and here he can flitter about like a wasp in the killing jar for all eternity, for all I care."

He vanished again.

Randt turned back to the crowd, eyes searching . . .

* * *

The auto-rememberer network stretched out like the root system of some insidious plant, invading every niche and cranny of the construct. Cleaver prepared to appear in the main street of the town, to block the escape of those assembled. Calwin stymied him—priority!

Again he tried.

Again he was stopped. In the darkness the two, now so well remembered, struggled for the same stations—stalemate! Neither sharper could break free.

Time passed.

Sheep grazed, trees lost leaves . . .

All the people had long ago left an empty construct.

Eventually Calwin relented. Cleaver appeared upon his throne overlooking his empty domain.

Calwin appeared next to him. "How does it feel to be lord of all that you see and master of nothing?"

Cleaver didn't reply at first but a grim smile passed across his lips. "If I am to be so fated, then it is only fitting that you too should join me in this long vigil."

Calwin shook his head. "I will take my chances upon the ground."

He changed aspects—he now stood in front of Cleaver in his saffron shirt, the lightning discharger in his hand.

"You relinquish the rememberers?" Cleaver seemed amazed at this turn of events.

"I do," Calwin said, and deposited three bloodied fingers on the ground before him.

"All yours," he said, and without further ado turned and began to run down the hill.

Cleaver's voice followed him like a wave. "Run, shopkeeper," he called, "for I am coming after you. Everywhere you turn I will be waiting."

I know, Calwin thought to himself grimly, *but I have one last card to play, one last trump.* He ran on . . .

* * *

At the base of the hill where two paths intersected, Cleaver was waiting, as he had known he would be. Calwin slowed to a halt. Cleaver had prepared: his white shield was positioned out in front, he was ready for anything.

"The lightning discharger will not help you for long," he crowed. "Its energy will be spent after less than half a dozen exchanges, and only the first few can do serious damage. What say you to that, shopkeeper?"

Calwin just shrugged and tossed the staff aside.

"Goodbye, Cleaver," he said simply. "Happy eternity . . ."

And then he was gone.

Cleaver, puzzled, waited for his next aspect to appear.

And he waited . . . until it at last dawned upon him that Calwin was right.

He was alone.

* * *

Calwin, however, was in the melt-mists; the green fog was all about him. Aspect-retrieval provided him with the two metre square patch of reality, and as he moved forward it replicated it again and again. As he moved through the mists, his aspects constantly changing, shadowalking, one Calwin after another threw his head back and laughed.

* * *

Calwin knew he had one final, perhaps unpleasant task—the twisting house's spiral doorway. About him the mists curled and twisted into primitive approximations, but they remained ignored as he concentrated instead upon the space in front of him. He usually called up the specific memory of his construct's interior wall, with its intricately designed ideographs, so that he could step directly into it. This time . . .

He was in the spiral—a glass panel, he put his shoulder into it—another, he was sprayed in glass. A fist through glass, blood spurting—like dominos now . . . He was falling through broken, shattering glass—his rememberers moved him on. He was crashing through broken, cutting glass—his rememberers moved him on. He stumbled through collapsing, shattering glass, he fell—the rememberers . . .

VII

IF CALWIN WAS STILL A tall man with reddish hair and blue eyes, then he would be satisfied. His auto-rememberers tracked him with loving detail, even down to his wounds, which had begun to heal. As he passed through the workshops and storerooms of the lower levels he thought now of what he had brought back with him, and of the consequence, of how when exiting the collapsing twisting house he had found only the Tollard waiting for him, like an obedient pet, and in its hand a note—three words, just three . . . My construct, please!

He had de-customized his rememberers.

If ghosts they were?

There was something there, he had to admit. Certainly the auto-rememberers, containing them in the lower level, had begun to switch more and more often, as if becoming the playthings of an inquisitive child. One thing he had decided on, however; he'd disconnected the killwire and stored it out of harm's way.

Just in case.

Clanwraith's Spiral

THE PLACE I FOUND MYSELF in was full of cages. The things inside the cages watched me silently with a variety of eyes, both number and size. The silence, I reasoned, would only be short lasting, so I took advantage of their surprise by stepping off the spell-bridge, tugging a green cloth bag behind me; it scraped along the cobbled floor as the things within shifted weight. Immediately the throng of caged familiars set up a whistling, hooting, screeching cacophony, designed not only to alert their master, but frighten the intruder.

I muttered to myself in irritation, damning the unpredictable nature of the spell-bridge and trying to orient myself with what I already knew of Clanwraith's tower, which was little enough. I had obviously entered an area under the spell of the protection wheel, for already I was suffering the subtle blurring of my senses which indicated its presence. I adjusted my spectacles to make sure that the confusions of my left eye were not repeated in the right. The special lens, so lovingly created by my master Malicorn, left me free of enchantments, or so I had been assured; it would overlay the protection wheel's fantasies. It showed a candlelit room full of cages and grotesquely carved pylons; archways led into other rooms, other mysteries.

I moved quickly to my left, and into the fantasy of an open and airy forest. The sound of birdsong filled the air, creating a problem I hadn't before considered. The protection wheel obviously worked on many levels. Both sound and smell told me I was in a forest, not in Clanwraith's tower, and although I could still see the frantic figures of the creatures with my right eye, their odd assortment of mouths were working soundlessly. Somewhere in this unlikely forest a frog was croaking, a deep throated sound like the tolling of a distant bell.

I stepped into another room. This one contained a strange array of helms lined up along a vast table, as if a banqueting group of knights had left them behind, but with their heads still within. Well, something was inside them, for strange shadows moved behind grills, yellow light flickered in the eye slots. I almost expected their headless owners to return and collect them.

I passed on, unnerved, half convinced that my lens was malfunctioning. The protection wheel provided a cobbled pathway that meandered its way between great trees. There were no more bird calls; the forest had become suddenly silent.

"They send the dead against me now," a voice said softly.

I turned around. The pathway had split itself in two, and at its intersection a scarecrow now stood. My right eye also detected something standing there, but it was indistinct, a collection of shadows and refracted light.

"You're either in the tower or in the maze," the scarecrow said.

"Is that a statement or a question?" I asked, reaching into my bag and withdrawing a small segmented mirror. I darkened the outer sections leaving only its central panel—a moon-haunted reflection of myself stared back, pale faced, skin drawn tightly across bone, silver coins for eyes. The duck egg blue of my robes contrasted with white skin and jet black hair. I felt like a china figurine frozen forever in some magical shop window.

"Why did you come here?" The voice was deeper now, hypnotic in tone.

Conjure man, I thought in reply, *Malicorn!* My image faded from the mirror. Its replacement, a bloodied hand holding a firebrand, grew in size as if moving nearer.

"Viel Partis," I called. And with this the outer sections of the mirror caught fire—a blinding white light. I was struck a glancing blow and stumbled sideways. There was at once a stabbing pain along with a certain numbness, but I did not relinquish the mirror. Again I was struck and this time the object fell away, dropping at my feet. I was vaguely aware of something large breaking apart, pieces flying about. Eventually I darkened the outer segments again—the hand holding the flaming brand retreated, while nearby there was a smell of charred flesh or fur, which not even the protection wheel could disguise. Lastly I noticed that the scarecrow too had vanished. Straightening my spectacles and grabbing my bag, I moved deeper into the tower. The protection wheel's enchantments remained.

I was standing at the edge of a shallow but swift-running stream. As I forded it, I could feel the cool water against my skin, the tug of the current at my robes. *Amazingly real,* I thought, as I plunged back into the forest on the far side of the stream, arriving next in a hall of shields and swords. Here unseen flames were reflected in burnished metal—shadowy figures moved on the flagstones and against the walls. Candles set back in alcoves flickered weakly.

I heard the sound of hoofbeats, and in my left eye was a golden-helmed knight on a white charger bearing down on me, sword swinging. A muddied path had suddenly appeared between the trees. I was about to dive to the side when I remembered and stopped myself—the sword passed harmlessly through me and the horse and rider followed suit.

Darkness was coalescing in the shields. As the fires died down, I caught glimpses of other things reflected in them—faces.

"Conjure man," I called to the mirror, "Malicorn."

As darkness passed across the moon that was the mirror's central panel, I saw the knight turning his horse for another charge, but it was different now, yellow light flickered beneath his helm. Once again I heard the dull thumping of hoofbeats, the hooves seeming to rise and fall in slow motion.

"Malicorn," the faces in the shields seemed to call, mimicking my own cry.

The moon returned as a crescent sword, and brandished by a bloodied hand it emblazoned the outer sections—moonbeams reached upwards. The knight swung his sword again. I flung myself away in a frantic attempt to escape the killing thrust. I took a glancing blow to the shoulder. In the sudden shock I dropped the mirror—it shattered. I screamed as my right eye caught a glimpse of other swords detaching themselves from the walls.

"Die!" cried the faces in the shields.

The knight, reinforced by his fellows, steadied his steed as they massed for a final charge.

Moonbeams played against the shields; they danced as the faces within twisted in sudden pain.

"Conjure man," I whispered in sudden hope, while more moonbeams gathered to my right eye, illuminating the lens with a fine tracery of cracks in the shape of a pentacle.

One of the swords was flung at me, as if by an invisible hand. I stepped to the side, as on high several shields exploded. Some of the swords were immediately brushed aside. Another flashed at me, but with less venom now, and it fell harmlessly away. Others were dropping, as the force that held them dissipated. I picked up the sword which had fallen closest to me, and noticed with a shiver my hand that gripped its icy cold hilt was covered in blood.

The knights now lay broken on the muddied path, their bodies fading even as I watched. Soon only their helms remained, but now not even shadows moved beyond their grills.

Moonbeams surrounded me, encloaked me, and the pain in my shoulder began to decrease. Encouraged, I pressed onwards, the forest closing in around, the sky darkening—I felt the protection wheel entering a new phase. It began to rain and I felt the first touch of dampness on my head and arms. Soon enough the rain became torrential and a film of moisture started to collect over the lens of my unprotected eye.

Up ahead I caught sight of a small cottage. *Another test*, I thought; Clanwraith's seeming intention not to show himself lent a distant nature to our battle. As I approached the cottage, I could see that a winding overgrown pathway led to a front door slightly ajar. *An invitation, if ever there was one*, I thought—*come in out of the rain and get warm!* Indeed I did feel cold and wet. That I knew it was only the protection wheel's fantasies made little difference; my body had been fooled into acting in this way and

I seemed unable to override it with logic. Swinging my bag over my uninjured shoulder, I pushed the door with the point of my sword, and entered a room dominated by a tapestry.

At first I thought the protection wheel had failed. In the darkness of the room, alleviated slightly by Malicorn's moonbeams, the tapestry depicting a prince-like figure could be seen. Unconscious and bleeding, the prince was lying on a donkey cart, surrounded by hundreds of broken swords. Another figure, unmistakeable as Death, led the horse, and wraithlike creatures trailed behind. Exactly the same scene greeted my other eye, so for a moment the unity of vision was as confusing as the fantasies, which had slowly been growing commonplace. *A trick*, I thought, or had I passed out of the range of the protection wheel? Too early to tell, I reasoned, and approached the tapestry for a closer look. It was a disconnected scene in a sea of black. The room/cottage appeared to have grown in size, so I had no feeling of being enclosed; the walls of Clanwraith's tower might as well have been rolled back and away, to leave me in this place, this abyss. Here there was only the tapestry. Laying down my bag, I reached out to touch it, and withdrew in shock as the scene dissolved into ripples. *This is not real*, I told myself, but my eyes saw it differently. As the water settled, the scene changed. A dark-haired, pale-faced man with oddly glowing spectacles looked up at me, sword in one hand and a green bag beside him. As I watched, the things inside the bag shifted weight and something fell out. I reached for it in puzzlement, wondering how it had got there; I certainly didn't remember packing such a thing. It was the body of a stuffed cat; where its eyeballs should have been, green jewels glowed with a sinister light. My grasping hand found only cold air.

Somewhere there was laughter. Pulling myself together, I looked back into the depths—moonbeams from my right eye passed across the face of the abyss like ripples. My deceitful reflection vanished.

There was movement within the darkness, like the turning of a great panel. There was a shuffling that might have been ancient feet—autumn robes disturbing dust motes.

I swung the sword—the mirror shattered, spraying me with glass fragments. I turned away, grabbing for my bag and stumbling into darkness. I crashed into something unyielding; it felled me and caused me to lose hold of my sword. Worse still, it dislodged my spectacles.

* * *

I was on my back in lush pasture. I lay still for a moment, staring upwards into a pitch black sky split intermittently by splinters of lightning, rain pattering against my face. I levered myself into a sitting position and glanced around uncertainly, still feeling groggy. A roll of thunder passed overhead like a receding wave. More shards of lightning split the night sky, illuminating briefly the shapes of other figures sitting miserably in the rain. The first, a wild-eyed man in the tattered remains of what once may have been expensive robes, sat fingering the well-worn hilt of a short bladed dirk—drawn from a long-rotted ceremonial scabbard. He seemed unaware of my presence. The second, even more unusual figure, sat hunched, an oddly cowled head cradled within arms extended by fabric or leathery skin. The overall effect was of a self-contained tent, off which the raindrops rebounded as if positively repelled—the picture of defeat and resignation was, however, the same.

I reached about with my free hand in a frantic search for my lost spectacles, feeling uncertain if I would even be able to distinguish their touch, such was the totality of the protection wheel's spell. I turned instead to my bag, and was reaching within, when the knife man jumped to his feet and pointed in the direction of the ruins of a great tower or cathedral, that had appeared in a lightning flash—its distance from our present position was difficult to determine.

"The tower," the knife man called. "I saw the tower again."

At this, the one I had come to think of as a night flier, raised his head—there was a look of infinite weariness in his gaze.

"How far?" he asked in a quietly desperate voice. The hawkish-nosed face was hard and weatherworn.

"Closer than before," the knife man enthused. "I was able to make out some of the windows."

"And the watchers . . . ?" the night flier questioned.

"No." The knife man shook his head. "The tower was in ruins."

With neither of them aware of my presence, I decided to try and make contact. "Are we in the tower or the maze?" I asked uncertainly, thinking of the scarecrow and waiting for their reaction. There was no response!

I understood now the hell into which I had stumbled. So many others must have come here trying for Clanwraith's tower and instead been broken and defeated; yet the worst was still to come, Clanwraith's protection wheel had an eternal nightmare lined up for each and every one of them—a spital of torment served up as entertainment for ghouls. I at last understood the meaning of the tapestry, for here then was the ultimate fate of the prince of swords, to battle for eternity in this theatre.

The lost souls of the knife man and the night flier had come to a decision, and were now making their way, albeit slowly, out into the storm. The night flier, when standing, revealed a hitherto unnoticed injury to one of his protective membranes. It hung piteously by his side, as he limped ponderously behind his companion who, with madly staring eyes, led them out into the darkness and the rain. I called after them several times but received no response, nor in truth did I expect one; here the protection wheel was king. I caught a last look at the tower, as lightning flashed on a distant horizon and then it too was gone— the rain pelted down harder than ever.

I took from my bag a collection of four small sandalwood sticks with peg-like attachments, and pushed them down into the grass until they formed a neat square about me, visible only when the increasingly violent flashes of lightning revealed them.

Taking a sacrificial dirk from the bag and transferring it to my belt, I turned the now empty bag inside out, revealing a totally black interior, as if the bag had vanished into itself. I stepped outside the square and attached the edge of this silken darkness to the pegs.

Would it work? I wondered. Such a magic snare, Malicorn had assured me, would sweep up enough of the protection wheel's enchantment to create a small breach; it would then be up to Malicorn himself to send through some indication of the spectacle's position. It was only an outside chance at best, I decided, but at least it was something.

I reached down into the blackness, searching for the reassuring touch of flagstones, but to no avail—I was grasping at formless shadows. I felt a prickling of my fingertips, as if they were brushing across sharp-tipped spears, and then they were entangled within a substance that felt like spider silk. My mind started to create horrid possibilities, but I refrained from withdrawing my hand in reflex horror. It was only the enchantment, I told myself; the protection wheel's layers of deception ran deep.

Suddenly my hand was grasped by another's. The tug was so strong it nearly made me fall head first into the bag, but not quite. I steadied myself with my other hand, braced against the sodden grass and attempted to pull back—my arm slowly withdrew from the blackness, and I noticed uneasily the blotches and blisters that now covered its skin. Had I placed my arm into boiling water?

I thought I could see something in the darkness, now being drawn deep from within the abyss.

"Viel Partis," I called at last in desperation.

The snare was the surface of a moon-haunted pond. I pulled the thing to the edge, a swollen and bloodied hand grasped around my own. Still I pulled—a second hand emerged, wrapped around the hilt of a long and glowing sword. Its head broke through the snare now—a terrible sight—Malicorn. In truth I had never before seen this aspect of my master, and I wished now that I never had. I turned my face away but still I pulled. Blue fire coiled up my arm like released serpents; moonbeams plucked at my eyelids. Malicorn rose slowly from the dark, and then the pressure upon my arms and legs was gone, the strain departed.

I was standing in front of my snare, with the magical spectacles dangling from my left hand.

Malicorn's image was all around me; it played in the mirrors—a shattered portrait, a ballet of disconnected body parts.

Drained and uncomprehending, I replaced my spectacles, but the images remained. I saw my own face split down the middle. The protection wheel? *No, I'm in the maze*, I realized.

Shapes coalesced in the mirrors—shadows. I reached out towards my own reflection—a hand appeared before my right eye.

An army of bloodied swords moved within this crystal chamber—a series of endless, interlocking, many-faceted surfaces, along which the trapped soul may traverse for ever. Malicorn had found his pathway to eternity after all, though how happy he would be about it was yet to be seen.

I reached out for my snare, but found only unyielding glass—a trickle of blood flowed.

In the mirrors, the sword was swung again and again.

I Am The Guardian,
I Must Stop You

I

SOMETIMES THE GREEN FIRE MANIFESTS *itself as a ship. The fire is the ghost of the ship, the part of it that always remains, only sometimes the ghost ship reaches out and finds reality—for a time the real rigging appears, the deck hardening from grey melt-mist into knot-holed, well-polished, foot-worn wood.*

Calwin the sharp-ghost twists and turns in his sleep. The voice a memory, and yet one he cannot place. Part of him delves back into old conversations, re-living and replaying, attempting to retrieve a memory from amongst those stored. The sleep of a sharp-ghost is not that of a final aspect; dreams there are certainly, and periods of restlessness, but there are differences too. Calwin sleeps the sleep of his construct, his mind brushing up against its storerooms and workshops, feathering its outer walls; an invisible presence, neither yet fully awake nor totally unconscious, but still in communion with his world. As he sleeps his construct hums with life, its outer disruption fields—walls of blue fire crackling as they dissolve the drifting melt-mist coming into contact with them—while deeper in, his involuntary spasms of movement are responsible for ghostly reactions in his construct. Here a remembering machine, switching itself on at random, rediscovers a door. Here a passageway suddenly aligns itself north-south when it had been east-west; consequently rooms closed off are suddenly opened. Things in his workshops vanish; other things appear. He begins to settle. The construct quietens with him; his remembering machines return to stable.

Outside the melt-mist sweeps up against his construct in waves of grey-green decay; dissolving mist, brushed aside for now by the disruption fields. In the street beyond, other disruption fields indicate the presence of other constructs. The street, Monserat Parade, main thoroughfare of the Uncertain Areas, one of four streets and by far the oldest and longest remembered, its wide flagstone paved presence ensured by the rememberer station that has given birth to it. Starholder's folly, some from Rimora had originally termed it, but other stations have dully followed, and in time more are planned. The first remembered road leads in one direction, to the greater disruption field that is the buffer wall for inner Rimora—Starholder's realm—while the other end loses itself eventually in the outer chaos of the melt-mists. Before then it is crisscrossed by three other stations and their resulting roads—Avatar, Fallstaff and Sternguard crossings. The sharp-ghosts are like the children of Starholder, tending to cling to their parent. And so too do their constructs; as yet, those outer two streets remain unpopulated and unpopular.

* * *

Calwin slumbers. Sixty-four sharp-ghosts do likewise.

Melt-mist, in its aggressive nightly form, strives unsuccessfully to find a gap in the defence, a weakness in the disruption field; but there are other things in this night, other more potent forces. Something moves in over the Uncertain Areas, in the mists, a green crackling. It passes across Monserat Parade, the mist about it glowing. It narrowly misses several constructs, their disruption fields flaring up like fire doused with accelerant. Within them alarm systems brought to the very brink, settle back into their tolerance levels; things are noted, however. Inside the sharp-ghosts sleep on.

The green fire curtain creeps up Monserat Parade, the melt-mist surrounding it like green cloud infused with lightning; it drifts towards a construct larger than most of the others. Tendrils of green fire reach out towards the disruption field; it begins to react.

* * *

Still Calwin slumbers. Deep within him the voice remains unknown, as too the words. There is no time, no place—he waits for further incoming fragments. Something broken up, fragmented, is reaching out for him. He turns over in his sleep. Other things are hovering on the edge of his consciousness, older things and darker. He senses something coming for him. He is standing on the prow of a ship; around him is melt-mist, now the mist is clearing and he is surrounded by sand, the ship is caked in it. He shields his eyes and scans the desert horizon. There are darker shapes dotted amongst the dunes. Sunlight plays upon them; he sees in shadow and reflection the mirrors—a graveyard of glass. They are shelved into the sand like tombstones. And then they are gone, and the mist has returned; but still the ship remains, and he upon it, holding something now—a mirror shard. It goes with him as he turns back into elemental form. Green fire crackles in the shape of a ship—soon only the green fire remains.

Calwin, released from his vision, surfaces at last, his construct-wide awareness stretched taut and nervy. Outside the green fire breaches his disruption field, and enters his construct's outer shell like a virus into his system. He awakens with a jolt.

II

RESPONDING.

Calwin feels as if he is falling. His bed is in the clearing of a forest, then in an unadorned room. His auto-rememberers provide him with a doorway. He rises hurriedly, attempting to regain composure, then stands for a moment, his auto-rememberers shuffling aspects. He chooses his battle dress, a cloak of blue with golden acorns. He vanishes and reappears, suitably attired. A tall man with reddish hair, he leaves his bedroom and has the rememberers rediscover a blank wall behind him. Everything may need to be sealed off, he thinks, though as yet he knows not what has penetrated his constructs outermost defence. He lets his construct awareness run through its analysis of the situation. A series of buffer walls have been retrieved and his outermost rooms, possibly compromised, returned to storage. His auto-rememberers provide him with a corridor and as he makes his way along it, heading in the direction of the insertion, he tries to imagine what has gone wrong. It is unlikely to have been simply melt-mist, as the disruption field is still intact; whatever has entered his construct has passed right through it. He thinks of the memory fragments that had filled his sleep, and decides that they must have a bearing on what is happening to him now. A green fire in the shape of a ship? Had that been what had breached his disruption field, and if it had, then how would his interior defences cope? Indeed, would they need to? Perhaps the insertion was accidental and ultimately unthreatening; certainly he shouldn't jump to conclusions.

Calwin comes to the end of the corridor and finds himself at his innermost buffer wall; beyond it three other such walls have been remembered, and laid down like obstacles in the path of his uninvited visitor. All the intervening rooms and their contents have been retrieved and placed into storage, so that damage can be avoided. But will the buffer walls hold? Calwin decides to get closer and see for himself. He causes the rememberers to retrieve the wall, and then moves forward into the resulting empty space. Ahead of him the next wall awaits, but already lines of green fire can be seen tracing their outlines across its surface. As he begins to retreat, the green fire begins to emerge fully-fledged through the wall; he can hear it crackling, but at this stage he still isn't sure if it is a ship. He causes the rememberers to return the fourth buffer wall, hoping in this way to at least slow its seemingly inevitable advance deeper into his construct.

* * *

Calwin, now in damage limitation, debates what is to be his next move. He could continue to remove all in the intruder's way, and hope that like some mindless magical virus it will simply continue to pass through his construct, and exit like it has entered, without fuss or damage. This is always a possibility, but he senses that he shouldn't count upon it. Close observation and continued wariness are called for, Calwin decides. If it does simply pass through, then he can consider himself fortunate; it isn't every sharp-ghost who can boast of such an insertion and live to tell about it.

Having retreated behind another remembered buffer wall, he suddenly senses a change happening; something is amiss, even more so. He waits for the green fire to emerge through the wall, but when it does, he notices the latticework beginning to solidify. As he steps back it seems to harden further. The front of the fire ship is nosing through the great wall, but its progress is slowing; it is being caught up. Calwin realizes what is happening; the fire is becoming real. The ghost of a ship is passing into flesh and bone before his very eyes.

* * *

"Good evening, Calwin," the observation device says at his arrival.

"Master, about this insertion," Calwin says, coming straight to the point, his concern overcoming the usual deferential considerations. "What are your thoughts, your ponderings?"

"Much effort has gone into preparing for such an eventuality," the observation device replies, "but there appear to be unpredictable developments in the insertion's propagation of itself."

"A ship is growing in my construct," Calwin emphasises.

"So it would appear," the observation device agrees.

"So what should be my next move?" Calwin asks.

"Complete isolation would seem the obvious course of action," the observation device says, speaking in Starholder's voice, his intonation and idiosyncrasy recreated to such a degree that Calwin once again imagines he is speaking to the original and not a copy.

"I've already instigated a complete retrieval of interior rooms and assets," he says. "The ship is floating now in emptiness."

"A black box," the observation device says approvingly. "You have done well."

Calwin feels himself genuflecting in its direction. "The ship is becalmed," he says at last, "and whatever magic created it, and brought it here, has so far made no attempt to show itself."

"This is to our possible advantage," the observation device theorises. "Whatever this insertion's true nature, it may only manifest itself under specific conditions. Whether these conditions have yet been met we cannot tell; perhaps it is merely being cagey."

"While it remains inactive, should I attempt to investigate?" he asks. "Or would I be better served to let it make the first move, always accepting of course that it isn't just some sort of magical relic."

"Magical detritus," the observation device muses, "a message in a bottle cast upon the tides, by creators unknown, and now returned by these same tides with answers possibly to mysteries old, magics forgotten."

"I take that as a vote for investigation," Calwin notes, smiling to himself.

"Investigation," the observation device agrees, "but with prerequisite caution."

* * *

Calwin decides to take no chances. With the ship of green fire hanging like some bizarre glowing decoration, in the black void that is now the centre of his construct, he knows that to use his auto-rememberers could be dangerous. Certainly he could have a passageway appear and allow him easy access to the fire ships exterior. But it could also give a possible entrance point to any ancient magic that might still be in attendance with the ship. He will have to use his aspect-retrieval system—his personal rememberers; being portable, they will allow him to make his way shipside without creating that possible bridge into his wider construct.

He prepares himself, running through a checklist; his aspect-retrieval system shuffles his remembered versions like a deck of cards. He appears in a chain mail vest, carrying a stave, then in a saffron shirt, then in his blue acorn version. He chooses these three from the menu and then disengages himself from the auto-rememberers. Three aspects! More than enough for the present jaunt.

* * *

The auto-rememberer removes a section of the buffer wall, and as Calwin steps through it replaces it behind him. He is in a void. The ship of green fire floats below him and slightly off to the right; seeing it now in its full glory leaves him feeling in awe. To begin with he hadn't realized how big it is, it is galleon sized, except that its rigging is green fire, and the sails are odd looking, great green pillows, deep and inviting; they pulse occasionally, like bellows. From this distance there appears to be no activity upon deck, but he doesn't know what may be hidden beneath. Time to get a closer look, he decides. A short shadowalk should suffice. He begins to move—his aspect-retrieval system shuffling his three versions expertly, the transferences as ever seamless. This constant altering, silver, orange and blue carrying him forward in incremental steps; in this way he closes in upon the ship. As he reaches its hull, he halts, and stretches out his hand; as he touches it there is no spark of released power, no unusual warmth or discernable cold, just an old wooden hulk.

"Seems real enough," he decides. "Time to consider the deck."

Aspect-retrieval lifts him, and as he rises up, floating almost within touching distance of the green fire; he half expects it to reach out and engage him in some form of magical transference. It crackles but otherwise remains neutral. He debates whether to go in closer and attempt something similar himself. Better not, he decides, remembering the observation device's warnings—prerequisite caution.

He looks down upon the decking, searching for some sign of a hatchway or an opening; there is nothing. Occasional rivulets of fire cascade down upon the deck, scattering and exploding like acid, skittering across the wooden planking and dissolving, as if causing a restrengthening of the whole. The fire is the ghost of the ship, he thinks, but this is surely an empty vessel; there is no one on board, if one doesn't count the green fire. Suddenly, however, he isn't so sure; on closer inspection, at the prow of the ship, the fire seems to be converging at a point. Something seems to be forming there, as if coaxed into life by his arrival. He watches intrigued, and perhaps a little afraid, as green fire plays about this form. It begins to take shape.

III

_____

IT IS AS IF THE ship of green fire is growing a crew, or at least one figure, the shape of a man, and he is holding something. The fire web is burning this tableau into existence, piece by fire-woven piece. Calwin begins to feel a sense of panic clutching at him. Time to leave, he thinks. He senses that the form is approaching totality, and he cannot be certain of what might follow. He remembers his vision, that feeling of darkness that had brushed up against him, and brought aspect-retrieval into play. He makes for the still distant buffer wall. But as he leaves the vicinity he feels something plucking at his rememberers, trying to disrupt him, as if attempting to understand the principles that underpin his existence. As he looks back, he sees a tall man holding a jagged mirror shard. He reaches the buffer wall and is allowed through—the invisible scrutiny ends. There is, however, a voice; the same one he had heard in his vision, the voice of the figure on the prow of the ship. It is warning him and calling for his help at the same time. He sees once again, in a fragmented glimpse, something falling through darkness, tumbling. But then he has reached the safe harbour of the buffer wall, and the contact is broken. He is undeniably shaken.

*   *   *

Calwin talks to the observation device.

"I was scrutinized by some form of magic," he says. "I felt it plucking at my rememberers. Indeed, I felt that it was actively trying to disrupt me."

"And the auto-remembered buffer wall?" the device asks. "Was it also effected?"

"I'm not sure," Calwin admits. "The wall seemed to settle into its place without any confusion, though whether its underlying structure was scouted I can't say."

"We may have to reconsider our plans," the device says, "put our investigations on hold."

"We scout it, it scouts us." Calwin says encapsulating the situation, "but who gains the most?"

"It does," the device said. "It is invasive in its nature, and therefore any possible advantages it can draw from us will only assist in its propagation."

"So you consider it hostile then?" Calwin asks.

"There is a high probability," the device replies. "Its actions are not consistent with that of a harmless relic."

"The mirror fragment," Calwin begins. "I sense the power there, though the one who carries it, I think unwillingly, tried to contact me. His voice is the same one that came to me before, when the insertion first occurred."

"We may have an ally in the enemy camp then," the device says, "or at least a wedge by which we may prise free this power from our midst."

"By comparison, the green fire seems a neutral magic," Calwin says. "When I approached, it failed to respond."

"A magic so old," the device says, "it can not be bent by other, perhaps even greater forces. It forms the ship, retains its memory in a way that I do not understand. Unfortunately this mirror form seems to also have, at some time or other, been able to manifest itself and become integrated. We must hope that it does not try to repeat the process with our systems."

"But you think it will?"

"I suspect so, yes. It has already formed some sort of opinion of us, just as we are currently doing of it."

"And if it thinks it has the stronger magic," Calwin says, "it might try to jump ship."

"Exactly," the device agrees. "It can't have been much fun, drifting for eons upon a tide of melt-mist. No doubt it thought it could have commandeered the ship, bent the old magic to its will, but instead it found itself going nowhere for eternity."

Calwin imagines Starholder himself, smiling at the irony of the situation.

"Now, however, it has been given a second chance by the vagaries of fate and the drifting currents."

"And we must deal with it," Calwin sighs.

"I'm afraid we must."

* * *

Calwin waits, his construct locked down and ready. He knows the move, if and when it comes, will not likely be a silken touch, more an urgent greedy violation.

He is right. Something comes blundering in upon his rememberers. Not a questioning touch, but a wrench—he feels his construct react. The auto-rememberers shift aspects, not retrieving yet, but shuffling furiously. Calwin attempts to hold the line.

Too late. A contained room appears like a lonely lantern, floating in the blackness of the void—the black box is compromised. Calwin attempts to return the room to storage. Once again there is resistance; eventually he is successful. Momentarily the pressure is released, the urgent probing ended. Calwin takes the opportunity to regain his composure. The mirror form has discovered the first layer of the auto-rememberer system and is exploring it. So far it is a random, unsophisticated search, but partially successful none the less.

The second attack when it comes is just as violent as the first, but far more sustained. Calwin feels as if someone is physically shaking him. The same room is hijacked off into the void; this time, however, Calwin's attempt to retrieve it is hamstrung by means he doesn't understand. His rememberers refuse to cooperate. A second room appears, then elsewhere in his construct, a corridor. Calwin tries again to regain control, this time trying to ascertain how the mirror form is overriding his system. It appears to be working in a simple, almost primitive way, but with vast reserves of power. He is reminded of a giant's fist knocking at the door, only this time it is rapping and it is relentless in its quest to enter. Calwin is rooted to the spot, his auto-rememberer fused; what can he do?

In the room about him the statue of a dryad appears, a painting upon the wall vanishes, a doorway is rediscovered. Calwin watches it all, unable to move, wondering when the invisible, still roving finger will alight upon him. And then realization strikes. He still has a chance—his aspect-retrieval system; he could go portable. Always accepting that the mirror form hasn't yet accessed the connections, but it seems so caught up in playing with its new toy he doubts if it has overridden his personal rememberer; he could attempt an uprising from the shop floor. Certainly it is worth an attempt! Calwin scouts the system, choosing only two aspects, and then disengages himself from the auto-rememberers.

* * *

All about him chaos rages. Calwin dodges about, as things come and go, in an increasingly manic expression of the mirror form's excitement at attaining such riches, after so long at sea. The room Calwin is standing in vanishes, replaced by his bedroom, sans bed; a work bench with boxes of varying sizes, containing melt-mist, stand in its stead. Things are being shifted out of their natural order. Calwin knows he has only a few moments grace, before the power that now capers about his construct concentrates its considerable force upon his probable enslavement. He has a mental picture of the figure on the ship, forever holding the mirror shard, and knows that to be his own fate if he is not to make the one final move left open to him. Intercede! Starholder's special remembered layer. He has never had need to access it before, but now he only hopes that it will retrieve successfully.
He accesses.

* * *

Calwin finds himself in a cottage in a wooded glen. He is sitting at the kitchen table, and the observation device is sitting across from him. At least it is an observation device; they all look alike.

"It would seem we are in quite a pickle."

"An understatement," Calwin says. "My construct is lost."

"Not necessarily," the device cautions. "This fragment of darkness, brought to us by the mists, will soon discover that when confronted by an equal and opposite force, the defining difference remains home advantage. I created this construct and its various elements, and will soon evict this intruder, never fear."

"But it has an intuitive instinct for unravelling unfamiliar magic," Calwin says. "We can only imagine what sort of journey it has undertaken, what things it has discovered over time."

"I too have discovered many things. And of time, I am confident that mine will have been spent at greater reward. Observe." The device indicates a space suddenly created in the air between them. Something is falling through the darkness, tumbling.

"The wizard in glass," it says.

Calwin can see now that it is a vast portal, rust orange; as it tumbles, shadows move within its depths. It comes crashing down upon the hard places below, in the darkness and the mist, fragments spraying out, scattering.

"And again," the device says, pointing to the space. There is a tower, a vast structure, surrounded by mist; but there is something happening, the magic stone is melting, the great portal, once loosened, begins to fall.

"You see," the observation device says, "this wizard born into darkness and mist will return."

A cage of blue fills the space, and when it clears Calwin can see an interior view of a section of his construct. This room seems deceptively normal, nothing vanished or changed. The scene alters, another room, this time a storeroom cluttered with various semi-magical devices, all now seemingly back in their original places. It is as if the chess pieces have all been returned to their starting positions.

"He is gone," Calwin says in realization.

"Not quite," the observation device admits. And a view of the ship of green fire as it still floats in the blackness returned. "But soon . . ."

* * *

Outside the melt-mist rolls up against Calwin's construct in waves, the night tide battering against its disruption field; burnt to smoke, it drifts away. Suddenly a section of the field fails, door-sized, the opening—melt-mist begins to enter the construct, as if sucked in through the neck of a bottle.

* * *

The black box is filling. Invasive melt-mist, flowing in, joins with the green fire and begins to mix as if a chemical concoction is being brewed; it starts to ferment. Calwin just wishes he could help the mirror form's unwilling accomplice—the ship's human aspect, who seems destined to hold the wizard's glass for eternity. As they go back into green fire, he realizes that there is nothing he can do. The ship begins to dissolve into mist.

* * *

The ship of green fire is now again in its elemental form; passing through the buffer walls and moving in accordance to some ancient unchanging instinct, it breaches the disruption field and makes its way back out into the night.

"It is unfortunate," the observation device says, "that these buffer walls were not stronger and retractable; we could have trapped the ship within a shrinking black box, possibly the size of a bottle. An interesting concept, don't you agree?"

Calwin imagines the original Starholder smiling to himself. "What about this melt-mist?" The stream of invading mist has halted with the disruption field's return. "It will soon begin to eat away at these buffer walls and damage the wider construct."

"There will not be enough time; the night tide will soon be over and the mist will return to its more passive form. Then we need merely disengage an auto-rememberer and you can empty the black box's contents outside."

"You want me to carry it out in aspect-retrieval? But surely the space limitations . . . ?

"You will need only the two aspects. I will simply recalibrate from number to size, allowing an infinite number of Calwin-sized aspects to be gathered into a single black box-sized one."

"You can do that?"

The observation device just nods.

*   *   *

Calwin stands at the intersection of Monserat Parade and Sternguard Crossing. Laid out before him the first remembered road makes its indomitable, yet doomed, way out into a vast and endless sea. Somewhere out there is the ship of green fire, and there are other things too, no doubt, just as strange and terrible. He thinks of a bottle bobbing upon dark tides, and wonders how many other such bottles there are. As he turns to go, he remembers and changes aspects.

Ashes to ashes.

Smoke to smoke.

Afterwards, he walks away.